THE ERIE MURDERS

JOHNNY MACK HOOD

authorHOUSE®

AuthorHouse™
1663 Liberty Drive
Bloomington, IN 47403
www.authorhouse.com
Phone: 1-800-839-8640

Published by AuthorHouse 1/13/2014

ISBN: 978-1-4918-5129-6 (sc)
ISBN: 978-1-4918-5128-9 (hc)
ISBN: 978-1-4918-5127-2 (e)

Library of Congress Control Number: 2014900181

CONTENTS

Chapter 1 – A Memorable Trip Begins   1

Chapter 2 – Meet the Gundersons   11

Chapter 3 – Muskegon   24

Chapter 4 – Manistee   34

Chapter 5 – Mackinac Island   40

Chapter 6 – Lake Huron   45

Chapter 7 – Dearborn, MI   50

Chapter 8 – Cleveland, Oh   53

Chapter 9 – Buffalo, NY   68

Chapter 10 – The Falls   76

Chapter 11 – The Hole Story   81

Chapter 12 – Into the Erie   94

Chapter 13 – An Erie Death   101

Chapter 14 – Into the Hudson   114

Chapter 15 – Manhattan   119

Chapter 16 – The End?   123

Chapter 17 – Arizona   132

Chapter 18 – Loose Ends   138

Chapter 19 – Postscript   143

CHAPTER 1 –
A MEMORABLE TRIP BEGINS

After their 'non' vacation in Colorado the Shelbys, JC and Susan, would probably such as soon not have met the Gunderson family, however, one cannot always chose ones chance meetings in life. They had had a pretty harrowing time in Colorado where they had planned a restful skiing vacation at an acquaintance's small ski resort near Aspen – well, at least JC had. Susan was not much for skiing either before or after the visit. She had managed to fall into a very precipitant gully at 12,000 feet elevation, coming through with a lot of bruises, a twisted ankle, a cracked pelvis and an exceedingly bad night in the remains of an old mining camp building. JC had had the luxury of a trip to Washington, a meeting with some very high officials, and a secret assignment that he was not even allowed to tell poor Susan all about. It was a difficult situation but one that they were bound to survive, and they did. Only now they thought they might have a little reprieve.

They had decided that after their whirlwind globetrotting adventures featuring murder after murder – all solved – more or less - it was about time for Susan to renew family ties and introduce her new husband, a specially created full lieutenant in the United States Navy, to her father and mother in Chicago. Poor JC who had started his short Navy career as an enlisted man typing and filing in a Navy office in Hawaii and suffering from acute chronic seasickness had never had much occasion to wear his glamorous new officer's uniform. But he had performed exemplary service and was widely admired for his sleuthing talents by commanders, captains and admirals from Washington D.C. to the Far East.

Little did his cheering section know that his sidekick and adoring wife might actually be the real brains behind this duo's success. It didn't really matter. Susan was happy enough to give him more than his due. She was delighted enough to soak up all the adventure that might come her way, mishap or no – and there had been plenty of those. She had long since quit dwelling on her drugging and kidnapping to St. Petersburg, Russia, the disastrous fall in the lava tube on the Big Island in Hawaii, or the cruise ship that had exploded beneath her feet. She did remember the most recent episode in Colorado clearly. She still hurt just a little and had to catch herself limping some from time to time. The doctors had assured her that would pass. This restful stay in Chicago with her family should go a long way in furthering her recuperation.

Susan had suggested she wanted to renew old acquaintances around the city and especially at the Art Institute where she had dabbled in some interests a bit more advanced than her high school efforts. It was from this background that she had progressed to a few courses at Avon College in Iowa where she and JC had met under peculiar circumstances. She had been working as a student assistant in the library when fate had drawn her with him into the investigation of a brutal murder in the stacks on the fourth floor. She had rescued JC in a sense from a brutal assault by the killer and had nurtured him to recovery. Love had bloomed and the two of them never looked back. Their joint efforts in sleuthing had paid off handsomely in satisfaction if not in money and had taken them to the far corners of the globe.

◊

All this running about, as much as she loved her hometown, was beginning to tire Susan. Her hip still hurt and she suspected she was really overdoing it. It was her dear father, Dr. John Beck, Professor at the Art Institute of Chicago, who could see the handwriting. Susan was not coming home for good. The old saying, 'how do you keep them down on the farm…' certainly applied to her. Besides, Dr. Beck and Susan's mother definitely approved of JC as a son-in-law. John Beck in his wisdom knew full well that strong-willed Susan would not be ruled by any husband, whomever he might be, and would march to her own tune.

So it was at dinner one evening that the senior Beck's announced at the supper table that they had a surprise for Susan and JC.

John stood at his place after finishing his dessert and said, "Susan and JC, Mrs. Beck and I have cooked up a little surprise for the two of you." He then gave Susan a fond look and continued, "Daughter, It looks as though you do not intend to spend much of the rest of you life sitting in a class room, much as your mother and I might have desired it at one time." He grinned as his look shifted back and forth between the two of them. "You two have seen a great deal more of the world than either your mother or I have ever seen or hope to see. For that we are both amazed and pleased, but there is one little bit of this old ball that you haven't seen, and you should." He gave a lengthy pause

JC and Susan looked at each other in puzzlement.

But then Beck continued, "Right here in your own backyard, dear girl, is some of the most interesting scenery and history that you will find anywhere – the Great Lakes Region…and I might add the Erie Canal and the Hudson River." He paused a moment and asked, "Have either one of you ever been to Niagara Falls, Buffalo, Manhattan?"

JC laughed, "I'm from California, you know. We have a nice bridge there in San Francisco – more than one actually - and the weather is good – better than the Great Lakes I hear."

Beck chuckled, "You are so right on the weather, but it is a beautiful and historic region and there is an awful lot packed into a relatively small area. But let me continue." He reached behind him to the sideboard and retrieved a brochure. He handed it down the table and said, "I have discovered an intriguing small ship cruise that departs from our own Navy Pier, traverses most of the Great Lakes, goes east on the Erie Canal and down the Hudson. It's a sixteen day journey and retraces a great deal of the early history of this nation." He smiled wistfully, "As an artist I would envy your first impressions of one of the great scenic wonders of this country and a subject of much early American art, the Hudson River. I wish I could experience it for the first time all over again."

To JC this was all a little bit of a puzzle. He had never given much thought to this region and he certainly didn't know that the Hudson River was so great. But, he thought, Dr. Beck is an expert so he must be right.

Mrs. Beck spoke up, "John was so enthused he went ahead and bought the tickets. I couldn't stop him. He insisted. He said if you didn't go he would take me instead, but I know you will both enjoy it." She then looked very seriously at her daughter. "You, dear, are not quite well yet and I worry. You have had too much running around here and I think a very good sit down on this nice safe little ship would be just what your doctor might have ordered if he had known about it."

Susan perked up when she finally absorbed the sitting down part of the trip. "I have to agree with Mom about the sitting down." She turned to JC, "I have connected with a couple of old school friends. I'm afraid it was disappointing. It's not the same as it was.

4

We've all gone our own ways. Let's give it a thought. We don't need to do any more sightseeing here."

JC Laughed, "A thought? I have a feeling that it is almost settled. The tickets are bought and I heard nothing negative from you. I'm game for a little rest too."

John Beck grinned, "Well, about that sight seeing – I have looked over the brochure and day one on the schedule has some sightseeing in Chicago, but maybe you can skip that if you're not interested."

JC asked, "Tell us about this ship. How big is it? Will I be bothered with my confounded sea-sickness?"

Beck pointed at the brochure that had made its way to JC's hand. "It's all in there. The ship is called the *Chicago Belle*. I think it carries about forty passengers. The company is based in Rhode Island and I read that it had been specially engineered to go down the Erie Canal. There are a lot of low bridges, I hear." He gave a really big smile, "JC, you won't be bothered with mal de mer. The Lakes are pretty calm most of the time – especially at this time of the year, and only in the old ballad about the Erie Canal are there weather related problems - fog. They do have a day at Niagara Falls. Have you two ever had a proper honeymoon?"

JC was feeling giddy. This was an enormous surprise and promised real fun for the two of them. "Susan dear, maybe we can get a two-place barrel to go over the Falls in."

She shuddered, "Not funny, sweetheart. I have a bad hip. Remember? I would like to see the Falls though. I've never seen them."

Things do turn out in strange ways. There was no mention of the Gunderson family. How could there be? That encounter lay in the future. They would surely have cancelled the trip had they had a crystal ball at that festive dinner table.

◊

Five days later, a Friday, John Beck and his wife dropped the Shelbys and their bags at the foot of the *Chicago Belle's* gangway on Navy Pier. Chicago's Navy Pier was built in 1916 and has served various functions over the near century of its life. It has been home to commercial exhibition halls, Navy training facilities, entertainment venues, and anchorage for WWII paddlewheel aircraft carriers. Today it is a Disneyland-like destination for tourists and locals alike and houses an enormous variety of attractions and features. Ships still dock along its two-thirds mile length and the concert hall at the end hosts distinguished musical performances of all kinds. It's a very busy and happy place in this midsummer season.

JC, the old salt of the group, looked up at what would be their home for the next two and a half weeks. The main deck had open lounging areas fore and aft and there was a row of windows partway down the main deck house that suggested they looked in on small guest cabins. The larger windows looking into the rest of that enclosed area seemed to give a view into the lounge or dining room. The whole ship had a peculiar flattened look to it. There seemed to be only that one deck with view access to the outside world. At the bow end was a small structure that would certainly be the bridge. The top of all this main deck structure consisted of a large flat space with a rail around it. Deck chairs and folding tables were visible. This was, no doubt, the sun deck. It could be quickly cleared for passage under low bridges.

At the foot of the gangway there was a small group of three young people dressed in white trousers and blue jerseys suggesting in their similarity of design that they were part of the crew. It turned out they were, and they were stationed there to welcome the passengers aboard and to carry their luggage to the on-board quarters. JC and Susan were saying their goodbyes when a group of seven mostly elderly people crowded up to the gangway more or less demanding to be boarded as soon as possible. Two of the group seemed to be in their late twenties but the rest were grey-haired.

The leader of the group was a small bushily bearded gentleman who somewhat imperiously announced to the gangway crew that they were the Gundersons and would they please see to getting them and their belongings on board immediately. The two young men and the young lady constituting the crew were happy to oblige and led the Gunderson tribe up the gangway and eventually into the neighborhood of a string of doors opening onto the narrow walkway that ran down both sides of the main deck outboard of the cabins.

◊

After boarding, JC and Susan managed to get most of their things stowed in the truly tiny cabin and then made their way to the lounge at the rear of the main deck.

Susan said just a little grumpily, "I didn't quite expect to be jammed into an average-sized closet, complete with washstand and toilet."

"Sweetheart," replied JC, "we won't be spending much time there I suspect." Looking off dreamily at the clouds he added, "I've had smaller in my illustrious naval career."

"I wasn't in the navy, JC. I haven't had the pleasure. Never mind. I'll get used to it. If I can get a good night's sleep at 12,000 feet in a ruined cabin I can make out on the *Chicago Belle* for two weeks."

When they entered the lounge they found most of what must be the passenger complement already there and seated around the room on the benches along the walls and at the tables. At the very rear were several comfortable couches with low tables in front of them, a regular living room arrangement. They guessed this would be where they would probably spend much of their waking hours; those hours not employed out on deck looking at the sights or off the ship on shore tours. They had hardly found a place when a tall, good-looking and rugged appearing individual entered the room from the forward center door.

"Greetings everyone, my name is Bob Walden. I'm the first mate of the *Chicago Belle* and will be your guide and explainer as we go along. This is a very small ship – it has to be to go where we're headed - and we have a small crew to go along with the ship size. You will meet the young people who helped you on board performing their many varied functions: cleaning, cooking, bottle washing, bed making and assisting on tours. They are all students from Brown University of Providence, Rhode Island on summer holiday; working holiday I'm sure they would insist." He laid a stack of folders on the table near his hand. "Here are the details of your time on board please come up and take one before you leave this room today. We will be serving a very light supper in this space tonight as a buffet. It will begin at five and close down at seven. Help yourself. Beer and wine are available from the galley. One of the students will help you with that. They are for sale at shore prices you will be glad to hear. Spirits are not available but if you want to dash ashore after this talk you can bring on your own bottle. There is a liquor store on the pier. Just put your name on the bottle and stash it on the ledge behind the couch there at the rear of the lounge. We have never yet had anyone make the mistake of drinking out of the wrong bottle.

"Let me now give you a few details about the cruise. Our captain is John Swain but we all call him Captain Jack and that is what he prefers. The only other full time professional aboard is our master chef, Richard Dockey. He spends most of his time in the galley making sure we none of us starve to death during the cruise. I think you will all agree by the end that he has more than succeeded. One of his special treats is a crusty loaf of freshly baked bread every day for the center of each of our dining tables. You may not all fit in your tiny cabins by the time we leave the ship. His food is that good.

"Now, we have an hour before eating time. Explore. The door forward behind me leads to a ladder that will take you up to the sun deck and another that will take you down to the lower deck cabins. Just beyond those ladders is the door that opens into the bridge. You are welcome on the bridge as long as you keep you hands off the steering apparatus. The water passages are very narrow at times." Everyone laughed. "Captain Jack is usually there – well, he is always there when we are underway" - more chuckles.

With that Walden smiled and retreated through the door behind him.

◊

The Shelbys took the time available to explore a little of the ship and to get their things stowed in their cabin which opened off the starboard side of the main deck. They discovered there were ten cabins, five on each side on this deck, and below, opening into a central passageway, were ten more. These lower cabins had small porthole views to the outside and were less expensive. Altogether the ship had accommodations for 40 paying passengers. They presumed the crew had quarters on that lower deck. Later they found that Captain Jack had a 'sea' cabin just behind the wheelhouse that he used nearly the full time he was on board. He also had a cabin below that he used mainly as an office.

Their own quarters were tiny by any standard – about ten by twelve feet – and that included a small corner with a curtain that enclosed the shower, washbasin, and toilet. They decided that at least they could leave the door open to the outside rail and pretend they had a verandah. Passing foot traffic along the passage might spoil the privacy of the arrangement however. The bed might be described as 'one-and-a-half,' instead of double or queen sized. They didn't mind. They loved to cuddle. In spite of all, it promised to be an interesting and happy occasion. One of their fellow passengers had commented in the lounge that he had heard the cook was excellent and that all could look forward to some of the best food served aboard any ship.

◊

After Dinner, JC and Susan took a long walk on Navy Pier. It was a fascinating and lively place at night – a sort of concentrated Disneyland. There were rides, Ferris wheels, booths selling everything, and a band playing Chicago jazz with some of the listeners actually dancing under the stars. Late in the evening there was even a fireworks display. They walked the full half-mile length of the pier and back. It amazed them to see how much could actually be packed into a mere fifty acres.

JC, being a Navy man and knowing a little about the Navy, was especially impressed by the pier's development. He said to Susan as they walked through the maze of attractions, "I heard that during the war they had two old side-wheeler lake cruise ships that were converted to training aircraft carriers tied up here, the Wolverine and the Sable. One of my Navy buddies said that they used them for training flyers before sending them off to the South Pacific."

Susan frowned, "That sounds somewhat hazardous – side-wheelers? You mean like they used to have on the Mississippi?"

"Well not exactly. They were pretty big and looked more like real ocean liners." He continued, "They were very hazardous operations. One guy said they have over fifty planes on the bottom of the lake out there," he said pointing to the east. "He said when a museum wants a World War II plane they just haul one up and restore it. The fresh water is a pretty good preservative."

Susan laughed, "And I'm the Chicagoan. You seem to have all the history well in mind."

The day finally ended and they both happily tucked in for the night eagerly anticipating a restful two weeks plus, beginning tomorrow.

CHAPTER 2 –
MEET THE GUNDERSONS

T he day dawned bright and sunny. At seven o'clock Susan and JC found themselves seated at one of the seven tables in the lounge for breakfast. The morning repast aboard the *Chicago Belle* was all one could ask for. Each table displayed an array of small boxed cold cereals, plates piled high with cold cuts and sliced cheese, and a loaf of freshly-baked bread with a large knife for slicing on a cutting board. There was a pitcher of milk available and a carafe of coffee. Guests were expected to serve themselves. The confusion of reaching for ones desired edibles or slicing the bread amid a scattering of crumbs was designed to promote getting acquainted among the gathered group. Each table was set up for six guests. The other four at their table were a major fraction of the Gunderson family that they had observed boarding the day before. Not much conversation ensued. The Shelbys introduced themselves and the Gunderson tribe responded. The young couple of the group and the older single woman were at another table. The Shelby's tablemates were Mr. Avery Gunderson, the apparent patriarch of the group, his brother Ed, and Jonathon and Myrtle Gunderson, Chicago residents. Jonathon and Myrtle appeared to be in their late fifties or early sixties. They overheard enough to discover that Avery and Ed were apparently from North Dakota.

There were no assigned table seats as was customary on a large cruise ship. On these very small ships people tended to gravitate into a particular bunching and seemed to stay that way for the duration. There didn't seem to be any rules.

Susan was delighted to be in the company of what she had decided were the most interesting group aboard. She nudged JC and said in a very low voice, "Fly on the wall."

JC frowned. At first he didn't understand what she was getting at then he became aware of what seemed to be a certain strained atmosphere amongst their tablemates. He gave a slight grin and nodded thinking to himself – *my darling Susan will find a mystery no matter what.*

During their meal they were introduced one by one to the young members of the crew. They visited and treated each table to a brief chat inquiring as to their needs during the meal.

The first to stop by was the young woman, "Hi, how is everyone doing? Can I get you anything – fresh coffee? My name is Lucy Goosey."

She abruptly cut off her announcement and stood grinning next to their table. The old man, Mr. Avery Gunderson gave her a wary look and frowned. Jonathon, the man from Chicago smiled and asked, "What an unusual handle. How did you come by that? Or should I ask?"

She laughed, "Oh you can ask – nothing naughty I can assure you. My colleagues and I are all from Brown University in Providence. Not unusual. Wait till you hear their names." She gave them a little wave as she made her way back to the galley. "You'll see," she called back, "At Brown we have certain ancient customs."

The other two crew had been making their way from table to table. One of the young men soon appeared, "Hi folks, the Gundersons and the Shelbys? Right? Let me introduce myself and tell you a little about our meal plans." He placed a platter of Danish on the table and then said, "They all call me Fender Bender. You can omit the last name and just use the first," he frowned and continued, "or more formally call me Bender – not to be confused with a robot of the same name on Futurama."

Myrtle Gunderson gave a laugh, "Certainly another Brown product? Go on. What about the meals?"

"Our main meal will normally be in the evening. During the day we will be underway on most days or on a tour ashore so we have to give the cook a break. You may meet him by the way. He's nearly always in the galley cooking up a storm for our next sitting. His name is Richard Dockey; we have made him an honorary member of the Brown student body and are calling him Dick Dock."

It wasn't long until a rather crestfallen appearing third member of the college contingent appeared. "I suppose my erstwhile colleagues have stolen all my thunder so I can only rain a bit on your parade." He was empty handed and seemed ready to weep at having nothing to do for his patrons. "I have the sad duty to announce my name so that when you call will you please call properly. I will appear instantly – or nearly so. I am addressed as Up Chuck. I would normally prefer everyone use only my last name, but my effort to instill that rule has failed so far." He then put on a patently phony long face and said, "When we tour you may not want to be sitting just in front of me on the conveyance. As a child my mother said I had a tendency to become car sick. Hasn't happened in years." He then smiled, "Please have a pleasant day. I'll see you all for dinner. Lunch will be sandwiches and drinks from a simple buffet here in the lounge."

Susan remarked to Ed Gunderson who was seated to her right, "That was quite a performance. Why all the odd ball names."

Ed replied, "I'm not sure. Someone once told me that some of these Ivy League schools have some peculiar customs." He turned to Myrtle, "Do you have a clue?"

Myrtle laughed, "Jonathon here used to do a lot of business with firms in New York in connection with his Chicago Transit work." She turned to her husband, "Have you got the answer, dear?"

Jonathon grinned, "All I know is that Brown is a very old outfit and some say they do indeed have some peculiar habits but I don't know anything about them. Maybe we'll learn before this trip is out."

Throughout all this exchange the old man, Avery Gunderson, sat impassive as a stone statue with a distinctly disgruntled look on his face. The Shelbys both came to the conclusion in their minds that although he was the patriarch of the family and apparently the sponsor of this delightful holiday for the seven of them he was really not much fun to be around.

As they were finishing their meal the door forward opened and the first mate, Bob Walden entered. He raised his hand and got the attention of all the passengers. "Ladies and Gentlemen, Welcome to your first day on the *Chicago Belle*." He laid some printed material on the table at the forward end of the dining area. "Here is a description of the day's activities. Each day I will post this plan on the small bulletin board you see behind me on the wall. Use that for reference during the day. If you want your own personal copy for a souvenir let me know. Otherwise, to save having more scrap paper around, I will post just the one.

"We will cast off and set sail in about thirty minutes. Our Itinerary today will be a brief cruise in the vicinity of this great city. Chicago is reputed to be one of the most architecturally beautiful cities in the world. It is best seen from the water and we will spend the better part of the morning and early afternoon having a look at the Chicago skyline from out on the lake and from the river. This ship is pretty special, designed to be able to pass under some fairly low bridges. This will allow us to do a short trip on the river and give you all a view of the sights close up. Ships this large normally have to confine their sailing to the lakes themselves. However, as you all know, and it's probably the reason you are with us, we have to navigate the old Erie Canal with its sixty-seven low bridges and we need this low profile. I shouldn't have referred to it as the *old* Erie. Actually the canal is greatly enlarged and improved over the old canal which you will be able to spot from time to time alongside our route. Late today we will be underway for our first stop on the east side of the lake, Muskegon, Michigan. It's about 110 miles and will take most of the night. It should be smooth sailing with not much to see on deck except the moon and stars. Feel free to hang out on all three weather spaces."

Susan wrinkled her brow and looked up at JC, "Weather spaces? What's a weather space?"

JC gave her a hug, "An old salt's term, it simply means an open deck, one that is outside and exposed to the weather. On this ship it would be the space up forward in front of the bridge where the captain or whoever is steering hangs out, the large deck that tops the lounge and the cabins like ours, and the rear deck outside behind the lounge."

◊

JC and Susan went to their cabin and changed into some casual wear for a day out on deck.

Susan asked, "Where shall we hang out to do our sightseeing? A lot of this is old time stuff for me but I know you will find it fascinating. Chicago is really a beautiful city and these shore line and river tours are extremely popular."

JC gave it some thought, "I've been thinking. Maybe we can split up and get acquainted with some of the other passengers. There are three other Gundersons we really haven't met yet, the younger couple and the single lady. Susan, that Gunderson bunch are an odd lot. I think we've got a line on some of them, at least the ones at our table, but those three might be worth getting to know." He shook his head. "That old man – Avery wasn't it – he's a bit hard to take. I don't think he opened his mouth last night or this morning. Just think we've got to put up with him for the whole two and a half weeks."

Susan laughed, "Don't worry. The rest of them seemed nice.

We'll get on okay. I don't imagine we have to keep our table seat for the whole cruise." She was quiet for a half minute then, "Do you know something, dear, we are acting like detectives again. Why in the world do we have to know anything about the Gundersons? There is a shipload of people aboard that we haven't even noticed yet. Relax. Let's enjoy the day at least."

"You're right," he said. "I'm going to park myself forward on that small deck just in front of the bridge. I might peek in there and see how Captain Jack does his thing."

"You do that," said Susan, "I saw some really comfortable seats at the back. I'll be there." She gave him a little kiss. "Habits die hard, don't they dear? We're splitting up as usual in the hopes of doubling our information gathering haul." She gave him an artful look, "No detecting. Is that right?"

JC smiled, "Mind your own business. I'm just off to see how they run this scow. I am a naval officer, am I not?"

JC made his way along the narrow outer deck passage to the prow of the ship. There were some benches there but most of the passengers had opted for the top sun deck, the roof of the main lounge and cabins below. That area had a removable rail erected around the perimeter, several tables set out under umbrellas, and plenty of comfortable folding chairs scattered around. JC looked up and could see that it was beginning to get crowded. Just behind the bridge was a door that opened onto a staircase that led up to the top deck. This stairway was also accessible from the central hall just forward of the lounge. He had a look into the bridge and waved a greeting to the captain and decided to leave him to his rather delicate chore of getting through the gates that separated the river from the lake.

They had all seen Captain Jack before but had not really had a chance to meet him. He was relatively young, a slender man with a black goatee beard and a natty looking moustache. He had a jovial look about the eyes but the humor that was undoubtedly there was kept under cover most of the time. JC concluded that he appeared very competent and was a man of few if friendly words. It was reassuring that he seemed all business. Everyone else aboard seemed to be concerned about nearly everything but the actual running of the ship. It was indeed a small crew, only two of which were actual sailors it seemed.

◊

As the ship proceeded very slowly into the narrow confines of the Chicago River Bob Walden's voice came on over a series of speakers strategically located throughout the ship. He began to describe the various buildings as they approached or passed them. And named the streets and boulevards whose bridges they passed under.

There were only four people on this small fore deck, one being the older apparently unattached woman of the Gunderson party.

She leaned on the rail next to JC and spoke first. "Are you and your wife enjoying the trip?"

JC smile, "Yes, uh – we've just begun though. Susan and I are looking forward to it. It is sort of a vacation for us. Her folks are Chicago people and they are treating us to this cruise." He was quiet for a few seconds then turning again to her, "I see you and several others all seem to be together. Is it a family thing?"

The woman laughed, "Let me introduce myself. My name is Maude Snyder. I am the sister of Jonathon Gunderson. I make my home in Manhattan. My husband passed away five years ago." Gazing out at the river for a few minutes she then added, "Old Avery decided we had to have a family gathering. This whole thing is his idea."

JC said, "I'm JC Shelby. I'm pleased to meet you Mrs. Snyder. That's very generous of him. Is the family very close?"

Maude burst out, "Ha! Close? I guess not. If we all had a choice I suppose none of us would be here. Avery says it's all Ezra's idea. Ezra was our uncle, my father Sam's brother. They're all dead now. Ezra was the one with all the money. His boys, Avery and Ed, have been running the business since he died. Avery does most of the running. I think Ed does about what he's told. Avery said he left very specific instructions about disposing of the property. This little soiree is the result. We were all commanded to participate."

JC was puzzled, "Commanded?"

"Sure. Avery says that Ezra wrote out a holographic will specifying that the property was to be sold when Avery reached the age of 77. How that old coot came up with that number we'll never know."

JC couldn't help but smile a little. This sounded like something out of a comedy. "So the family property is about to be sold and you are all off on a celebratory trip. Is that right?"

Maude laughed and turned to face JC. "Some celebration: I don't think any of us are here by choice. As for me, my husband left me well off so I could just as well stay at home in New York but Avery said no. He says it would violate the terms of the will or instruction, whatever it is, and everybody had to go along on the trip."

JC was beginning to feel just a little embarrassed and uncomfortable. He really didn't need to know all the personal history of a bunch of strangers.

"What is ironic," continued Maude, "is that one of this sorry lot isn't even here – Abe, Avery's twin brother. Avery says he's in Arizona and absolutely can't make it. If that doesn't violate the terms of the will I don't know what does."

JC frowned, "I still don't see why you couldn't have just stayed at home in New York."

Maude scowled, "Hmph! And do my young cousins from California out of six million dollars. They need it. I couldn't give it to them – or any amount for that matter." She looked up at JC. "Living in Manhattan costs a lot of money and I just can't afford to support them so I had to go along – see that they get their fair share." She turned away from JC and started down the narrow outside deck toward the door to the lounge. She waved over her shoulder. "See you later Shelby. I'm going in and get myself a shot. Bought some good stuff on the pier last night. Don't fall overboard."

JC scratched his head. What an encounter. He would have a little story to tell Susan later. There might not be a murder to solve but the voyage promised to be interesting.

◊

Susan was getting her own jollies on the aft weather deck. What she was about to find out about the Gunderson clan was bound to spoil JC's evening. It was a near duplicate of his information. The rear deck was considerably larger than the one at the bow and was sheltered by the lounge and dining structure. There was seating here for at least a dozen. Her hip was hurting so she found a comfortable lounge and settled into it. One of the young crew, Up Chuck, she thought, came by and sensing her apparent infirmity offered to bring her a drink. She ordered a glass of lemonade and thanked him profusely. This was her first time to really relax and watch the world go by, to her a familiar world. Seated next to her happened to be the distaff member of the young couple belonging to the Gunderson clan.

She was a bubbly person and began right away to break the ice, "Hi, I'm Clotile Darling, old Avery's granddaughter. That's my husband Darrell over there at the rail gawking at the buildings. You'd think he never saw a tall building before. My goodness we're from L.A. We have lots of tall buildings out there. So glad to meet you; I saw you at the other table having to put up with all the old folks this morning."

During the brief interval while she was catching her breath Susan said, "Hi Clotile, I'm Susan Shelby and my husband is JC. He wouldn't be happy if I told you what that meant."

This was red meat for Clotile. "Oh, I just have to know. I promise not to use it on him – much – or often." She broke out in a peal of laughter.

Susan had already had thoughts that this group could have a lot more in the interest line than they had first assumed so she went along with the banter. "Promise not to tell him I let it out."

Clotile put on a long face and said, "Oh yes. I promise," and then laughed.

Susan said with feigned solemnity, "Jeremiah Cuthbert."

"I promise never tell. To use –yes – but to tell – never," said Clotile.

Susan then asked, "What are you and Darrell doing here with all the old folks? It's a nice trip but wouldn't you have had more fun alone?"

Clotile screwed up her face and said, "Would you believe this is the seven million dollar voyage? Or six or something. A lot anyway." She leaned back and giggled. "Make a movie title wouldn't it?" She said, "Old granddad, that's Avery, is forced by some legal trick or other to sell off all the property in North Dakota and divide up the money with all the surviving Gundersons. I may now be a Darling but I once was a Gunderson. Good trade off, eh?"

At that moment her husband left the rail and came to sit with them. Clotile made the introduction and said, "Dare, honey, I was just telling Susan here that we are about to become very rich. I don't remember what the whole thing is all about but you do, don't you?"

Darrell was apparently used to his feather-brained wife's running on and it was clear he loved her dearly. "Yes, there is no particular secret. Old Ezra said that when Avery reached 77 he was to sell the farm, ten thousand acres of wheat, and all the machinery and buildings and divide the proceeds among the surviving Gundersons. It appears there are six of us – Avery, Abe, Ed, Maude, Jonathon, and Clotile."

Susan asked, a little reluctant to pry further into the Gunderson family affair, "What do you do in California, Darrell?"

Darrell Darling stammered slightly, "I, uh – do movie work. I'm an actor – uh – a producer."

Clotile cut in, "He's looking for something right now. We sure could use the seven million. Wow! Dare and I could just move right away to a better place." She turned to her husband, "Maybe Beverly Hills, huh, dear?"

Susan frowned and began ticking off on her fingers. "I get eight persons. I counted only seven in the dining room. Who is missing?"

Darrell said, "Oh that would be Abe. He's out in Arizona; couldn't make it; got some sort of legal exemption. The rest of us have to be here according to the will." He waved expansively, "so here we are."

◊

Sightseeing the shores of Chicago and the river views of this energetic and vital American city finally came to an end. The sun was low over the spectacular city skyline when Bob Walden made an appearance up on the sun deck to announce dinner.

"Folks, Dick has our repast nearly ready. If you would all like to have a drink before you eat please repair to the lounge. You have about thirty minutes. There are no assigned places so take seats wherever you like when we call."

Most of the passengers ferreted out their bottles from the various nooks and crannies in the lounge area where they had chosen to secret them. Glasses, mixes and ice were laid out on a table at the head of the dining space. As the cruise progressed nearly everyone found that simply placing their bottles on the window ledges behind the couches and chairs served in place of a liquor cabinet very nicely. Bob's suggestion was the right – and only feasible one.

Susan and JC tucked into a corner away from the crowd and compared notes.

"I had a very good talk with Maude Snyder," JC began. "She has plenty already and really doesn't need the money but apparently coming on this cruise is not optional." He scratched his head. "I just wonder how the brother in Arizona was able to get off the hook." JC smiled, "I like Maude. She is a piece of work; somehow doesn't seem to fit the mold."

Susan grinned, "If the mold is shaped to fit the Darlings it would result in a fairly amusing group. They are wannabes from California hoping to break into the movies." She frowned, "Somehow I don't see them fitting the image of successful movie people." Then she mused, "I don't see their money lasting all that long either. I truly believe that Clotile will manage to get rid of most of it fairly quickly."

JC gave a slightly crooked smile, "You know, it's none of our business anyway," then added, "but they really are an interesting lot. Jonathon and Myrtle are a fairly reasonable pair. Maybe that's what Chicago does for you." He grinned and gave Susan a squeeze. "I love Chicago people, specially this one."

Susan gave here husband an adoring look and said, "I love naval officers, specially this one."

◊

Dinner found them at the same table as for breakfast; Avery and Ed, Jonathon and Myrtle. A large warm loaf of crusty bread on a cutting board graced the center. No one seemed to make a move so JC grabbed the knife and began to hack the loaf into thick slices for the six of them. This resulted in a lot of crumbs and amused banter. Avery sat passively watching the procedure with a faint expression of distaste.

It wasn't long before the young crewmembers began to appear bearing platters of meatloaf and bowls of vegetables. A caesar salad was placed in the center and everyone was expected to help themselves. The whole procedure suited JC and Susan. Fender Bender commented in passing that this was to be the standard procedure for meals for the entire cruise. It served to break the ice and to start the conversations flowing. The food was excellent.

Near the end of the meal Bob appeared through the forward door to make an announcement. "Ladies and gentlemen, we are now on our way to Muskegon, a distance of about 120 miles. It will take all night with us arriving about nine in the morning. There is no hurry so Captain Jack will cruise over the smooth Lake Michigan waters at about eight knots. You should have a very restful night and views of the starry skies from on deck should be magnificent. Feel free to wander about. Be careful. Don't fall overboard." He laughed. "There is TV in the lounge area." He chuckled again, "Please don't fight over channels. We try to advise our guests that the news is not the most conducive to a pleasant vacation time but we don't dictate. Watch whatever you want." He gazed up at the overhead and waved his hand, "Me, I would prefer the stars and the moon, which by the way, rises about ten tonight."

CHAPTER 3 – MUSKEGON

A t nine AM the *Chicago Belle* was making its way through the narrow entrance into Lake Muskegon. The city of forty thousand surrounded the large body of water. On both sides were visible the residential waterfront neighborhoods, most with boat docks for private sail and motor boats. Muskegon was definitely a water-oriented city.

Bob's voice came over the speakers located on all the weather decks and in the lounge, "Good morning friends. I hope you all enjoyed your breakfast today and were able to get out on deck to watch our approach and entrance into Lake Muskegon. We'll be docking very near the downtown district. It's a relatively small city and should be easy walking for those of you that wish to see the sights and do a little shopping.

"Please be back on board by three this afternoon. We will get underway at four and be well out on the lake by dinnertime. You are on your own for lunch. If you choose to stay aboard, Dick, our gourmet chef, will have sandwiches and fruit available about noon. Have a very pleasant day. The weather predictions are for warm temperatures, partly cloudy and with a slight breeze from the southwest."

The Shelbys did decide to do a little exploring and made their way to the gangway on the lower deck as soon as the ship was tied up. The Jonathon Gundersons left at the same time.

As they set foot on the dock Myrtle turned to them said, "Do you two have any special Plans?" She gave them a broad smile. "We live just across the water, of course, and have been over here frequently."

Jonathon smiled and said, "We might walk along together for a little until you get your bearings. There are some interesting little shops – that is, unless you have some special plans."

Susan laughed, "Plans! No. Of course not. I'm originally from Chicago but I've never been here." Turning to JC beside her, "And this guy is strictly a California type and wouldn't have a clue about this part of the world."

JC put in quickly, "I think it would be great. We'll join you and you can show us the wonders of Muskegon."

This caused quite a laugh.

Jonathon said, "I don't think Muskegon qualifies in the wonder department. It is a nice little city however. If you own a boat it's ideal. A lot of Chicagoans vacation over on this side of the lake."

Myrtle added, "The only real problem is the wind. It comes mostly from the west, which makes sailing out onto the lake a bit of a chore. We're not sailors so it never bothered us. We just liked to come over to enjoy the small town atmosphere and the fresh breezes off the lake in the summer. We also like to take drives into the surrounding countryside. It's famous for their cherry orchards."

After a couple of hours of strolling through the business district the foursome settled on some benches on the waterfront with paper cartons of coffee that they had picked up at a nearby Peet's Coffee kiosk.

JC broke the ice on the subject of this peculiar family affair. "I understand that this is a rather unusual gathering of the Gunderson Clan."

Jonathon gave a crooked grin, "Unusual is hardly the word – 'bizarre' I would call it."

Myrtle broke in, "I guess you already know from some of our other kin folk that there is a great deal of money involved. The relationships are a little tangled. My hubby here and Avery are first cousins. Their fathers were brothers. Avery got everything from his father, Ezra. He was the one who left the crazy will."

Jonathon chuckled, "We didn't object. We can use the money but we don't really need it. I've had a good job with the Chicago Transit Authority. Frankly I don't see how we deserve anything. The farm and all those assets were strictly Ezra's doing. My dad, Samuel, worked for the Northern Pacific Railroad. He was not into farming. That's where my interest in transportation came from I guess. Anyway, it looks like we are in for a windfall. Avery is selling to ConAgra for around forty million. We get an equal share with each of the rest of the Gundersons." He hesitated for a space and looking just a little embarrassed continued, "Avery has done all the work. We really don't deserve it."

Myrtle's eyebrows went up. "Deserve it or not we get to do a few things we couldn't before – a little trip to Europe for example."

Jonathon gave her knee an affectionate pat. "Right you are sweetheart - off to Europe before the snow falls. Eh?"

Susan changed the subject slightly, "I understand there is a missing Gunderson. How did that happen?" They had talked enough about the family situation so that she was not embarrassed to broach what might be a delicate topic.

Jonathon replied, "That would be Abe. He's in the Phoenix area. The way I hear it he is not particularly well and his doctors have forbidden him the strain of travel. Also I understand he needs the Arizona climate to stay as fit as he is – which isn't much, I hear."

JC put in, "I guess the legal beagles were able to get an exemption on that."

Jonathon said, "So I hear. I really don't know anything about the matter actually. In any case there are six of us so we should each come up with about six and three quarters million before taxes, and

I haven't a clue about the tax situation. I presume Avery knows all the details."

◊

At four the last line to the dock was aboard and the little *Chicago Belle* was headed west out of Lake Muskegon. Everyone was out either on the upper sun deck or lounging out aft of the lounge. Most had opted for an early cocktail and the comfortable breeze engendered an air of mild excitement anticipating the sights and experiences that lay ahead. People were finally getting unwound from their frantic everyday lives and were looking forward to two weeks of pure relaxation.

JC was up on the sun deck and had taken the opportunity to talk to some of the guests that he and Susan had not had a chance to meet yet. She was down on the aft deck and had managed to collar Maude for a few words. JC had the thought that Maude being alone on this trip might like a little special attention and Susan had agreed to help out. It was no chore however. Maude was a charming, if somewhat opinionated and brusque; just the type that Susan liked. The stimulation of some contention was far better than the boredom of the book she had picked up in the lounge.

Time flew by. JC was talking to a couple from Salt Lake City when Bob Walden's voice boomed out of the topside speakers. "It's six o'clock folks; Dick has your dinner ready. Come on in and find your seats."

Everyone crowded the ladder leading down into the passage just ahead of the dining area and found their seats. There was a little shuffling around but most seemed to take whatever seat they had wound up with on last night's meal and this morning's breakfast. JC marveled at the herd instinct that seemed to prevail on cruise ships. These initial chance decisions seemed to inevitably stick for the whole voyage.

As expected, Susan and JC had Avery, Ed and the Jonathon Gundersons for table companions. The young students served the salads and managed to announce in passing that tonight was fish night, poached salmon.

JC asked Susan quietly, "Whatever happened to the fish from the lake?"

Susan gave a grin, "We still have local fish but tonight we have salmon. Don't complain. We may luck out and have whitefish before the trip is over. That's the best."

This was all news to California reared JC who had grown up eating tuna, mackerel, and various kinds of rockfish. The meal began without much conversation beyond a few quiet greetings on being seated. JC finished his salad and was about to begin on his fish course when he noticed what seemed to be strange behavior on the part of Avery Gunderson. He appeared to be in some distress. His face had turned quite red, to such a point that JC wondered at first if he was choking, then he paled and began to stiffen; all of this without a sound. None of his family seemed to notice at first. He hadn't said a word. JC finally began to seriously worry. Mr. Gunderson was in real distress. He stood up and leaned across the table.

"Mr. Gunderson, are you all right? Can I help you?"

Gunderson didn't utter a sound but began to slump in his seat. JC was panicked at first and then leaped back and went around to the old man's place. He shook him gently by the shoulder but got no response. He raised his head and shouted out as the rest of the table got out of their seats.

"Help! Somebody get some help. Mr. Gunderson is having an attack. It could be his heart."

The door to the forward passage burst open and Bob Walden came in on a run. "What's the matter?"

"Gunderson here is in trouble. Do we have a doctor aboard?" JC said.

Walden rushed to the man's side and took him by the shoulders,

"Shelby, give me a hand. We've got to get him below. I've got my medical kit in the cabin there."

JC said, "But we need a doctor."

Walden looked up with a grimace, "We haven't got a doctor. I have training though. First mates on these small ships usually have some medical training. It's required." He began to lift Gunderson gently from his seat. "Give me a hand here Shelby let's get him below. Hurry!"

Gunderson was of slight build and it was not difficult for the two of them to gently carry him forward and get him down the ladder to Walden's office. When they entered JC was surprised to see a medical cot in the corner. Apparently these ships did come equipped for emergencies.

Walden ordered, "Help me get him up on the cot then go back to the dining area and try to get people calmed down. There is no need to disrupt everyone's day. He'll be all right." He began to loosen the old man's clothes and then opened a case containing his medical supplies."

JC stood for a moment watching in paralyzed fascination as Walden prepared a syringe.

Walden stopped and gave him a look, "I'm okay here for now. Please get up topside and give people the news. I think we're going to be all right." He turned back to his task and then looked at JC again and said, "Step into the wheel house on your way and give Captain Jack a report. It's vital to keep him in the loop. When you get to the dining room tell the staff to get some music going on the speaker system. Make sure everyone has a drink or whatever they want. We can't have any panic just because one of our guests has had a spell." Just as JC was leaving the room Walden said, "Please close the door and tell everyone to not disturb us here. Mr. Gunderson needs to have it quiet."

JC's last glimpse of the old man was worrying. He lay absolutely still and looked awfully gray. He hoped that Walden knew his stuff. At the top of the ladder he went forward and stepped into the bridge.

The captain turned as he entered and said, "What's all the ruckus? Chuck stepped in a minute ago and said one of the passengers had had a heart attack or something."

JC explained the situation.

"You had better go on in then," said the captain. I can't do anything. I have to steer the ship. Bob is the only relief I have aboard."

JC asked, "Hadn't we better turn back or put in somewhere?"

"There isn't any decent place to stop until we reach Manistee in the morning. There's nothing can be done at this point. It's too far to go back. I trust that Walden can get him stabilized. If he reports no progress in the next half hour or so we'll give the Coast Guard a call and they can send a helo out. That's the best we can do. I will alert them as soon as you leave."

All of this sounded reasonable so JC made his way into the dining area and delivered the message. He sat down next to Susan and looked at his unfinished meal. He didn't have an appetite at this point. A drink would not go amiss but he and Susan had not supplied themselves with any spirits in Chicago or Muskegon and somehow wine or beer didn't answer the need.

Very quietly Susan said, "What's really wrong? Anything?"

JC shook his head. "I don't know. I have a funny feeling. It's a bit odd. I have no experience. Somehow it doesn't look like a heart attack but I don't have any real world experience."

Susan spoke to Ed across the table, "Did Mr. Gunderson ever have any trouble before?"

Ed Gunderson had been sitting in stunned silence ever since the event. He shook his head, "Nope. I've never seen Avery sick a day in his life. He's not very big but he is tough as nails. I don't understand this."

Jonathon Gunderson finally broke his silence, "Well Ed, with Avery laid up I guess that makes you senior around here. None of us know anything about the farm or Avery's business."

Over at the table where the Darlings were seated with Maude

the Gunderson contingent was particularly silent. Clotile seemed to have a slight smirk stealing on and off her face. Susan picked up on this and would later comment to JC about it. Strange! Lucy had served Maude a Manhattan, apparently made from a secret ship-owned supply of the hard stuff. In spite of soft music that soon made itself evident from the speakers the mood was distinctly morose. Everyone seemed to be downing their drinks but nobody was particularly enjoying them. The ship moved on and no word was forthcoming. The sun had set and, to match the mood aboard, it was growing dark.

Bender stood up near the forward door and said, "Let there be light - and better music." With that he put on more lively tunes and flooded the room with more light. He went on, "Hey – people fall ill on cruise voyages. This is not a disaster – except of course for dear Mr. Gunderson."

Maude could be heard mumbling at her place, "First time anyone ever called him 'dear'." No one raised any objections to the pejorative remark.

Although it was only thirty minutes the suspense seemed hours. The forward door opened and Bob Walden stepped in. he didn't need to speak. His face bore the message.

"I am very saddened to have to tell you that Mr. Gunderson has died. It was indeed a massive heart attack and nothing could be done. I have had a conference with Captain Jack and would like to meet with the Gunderson family at the back of the lounge for a few minutes concerning arrangements. The rest of you please continue your meal or whatever you were planning. The trip will continue. We are all going to have a very good time. These tragedies sometimes occur. On a small ship it seems to affect people more than it would on a large cruise liner but these incidents happen as a regular but unavoidable thing and we just have to soldier on."

The Gunderson clan rose from their seats and drifted to the couches at the rear. Walden joined them and perched himself facing them from a tall stool near the magazine rack. The Shelbys remained at their dining table with Susan all ears to hear what the first mate was going to say to the family. Her curiosity itch always won out over genteel manners.

Walden began when they were all settled, "Being the family all of you have a decision to make. We have a number of options. Mr. Gunderson's remains can be transported from Manistee to the nearest airline terminal capable of handling such matters. One or more of you might want to accompany him back to North Dakota. That could be quite expensive and of course would disrupt the trip for all of you. Or we could make arrangements for him to be buried somewhere in the vicinity of our next stop, Manistee. This might not be too easy to set up."

Jonathon interrupted, "Mr. Walden, let us be clear on this matter. Ed here is the only one of us that really has any relationship with Avery. The rest of us hardly knew him – or really didn't know him at all. We're sorry he passed away but let's keep it simple."

Maude put in her two cents, "It's Ed's decision. He can take him back or whatever. The trip is paid for and I for one would love to finish it."

The Darlings nodded vigorously at this.

Walden continued, "The last and maybe the best option then is for us to employ the services of a company in Manistee – a funeral services company I happen to know of – to take charge of the remains, cremate them and deliver the urn to the family either by mail to his home or back to the ship."

There was much nodding and whispering back and forth among the relatives of Avery until finally Ed said, "It's decided then. Cremate him at this next stop and let's get on our way." He smiled, "I haven't been off the farm for many a year and I for one wouldn't want to miss the rest of the trip either."

"One last thing," said Walden, "As medical officer of this vessel I have the authority and the obligation to sign the death certificate.

I need to do that for the authorities in Manistee. Meanwhile I will call ahead to have the funeral services company meet the ship at the dock. I need to make this all crystal clear for all of you." He hesitated for a few seconds. "Hearing no objections; that will be the procedure."

With that he went forward and disappeared through the door. All knew that he had work to do down below with poor old Mr. Gunderson's corpse.

After everyone had dispersed Susan urged JC to come back with her to their tiny cabin that opened off the weather deck just forward of the dining area. On her way she stopped a moment at their table and scooped up a napkin. As she made ready to leave the dining lounge she stopped at the Dutch door that opened into the galley. Dick Dock responded to her request and produced a Ziploc bag into which she dropped the purloined napkin. When they got to their quarters they both sat on their one and a half sized bed.

She actually seemed jubilant. "JC, sweetie pie, it's murder. I know it is."

JC in mock exasperation, "Susan, you are incorrigible. Every death on the planet is a mysterious crime to you."

Susan literally bubbled with excitement, "Look JC, you said yourself you didn't feel right about it. And motive – millions! First there were six to inherit and now there are five. And better yet we have only four suspects and they are all safely confined on this little tub." She gazed up at the very nearby ceiling. "All we have to do is sort them all out and bring the miscreant to justice."

"Susan, darling, you have just won the Olympic medal for conclusion jumping. Slow down. First of all you have to brush up on your elementary math. There are six left in the Gunderson party. Are they all suspects? Or only the ones that are related? Are you including or leaving out spouses? How about the crew? The captain? Might you include any of the other passengers?"

Susan gave a laugh, "Shut up, sweetie. You know what I mean."

CHAPTER 4 – MANISTEE

B right and early the following day saw the *Chicago Belle* making her way up the long narrow channel to the main dock in the center of the small city of Manistee, Michigan. An early loudspeaker announcement aroused all the guests and got them on deck for the arrival.

Bob's voice boomed, "Ladies and gentlemen we will be tying up at a small dock right in the center of downtown Manistee. You have quite a treat coming. Although small, Manistee is quite famous and has a wealth of tourist attractions. It was originally the world's largest producer of shingles, a large lumber port, and was home to several famous salt manufacturers. They say that Manistee had more millionaires per capita than any other place on earth. It's an unusual place with its museums, an opera house, and many other cultural attractions and only about 6500 residents. It is on the national register of historic places. We only have one day here and believe it or not you won't be able to take it all in. Oh yes, it's also the home of a film production company. We may be greeted by a group of citizens in costume, and most likely they will have the town calliope going for us."

Susan and JC ate a quick breakfast and planted themselves at the rail just outside their cabin to watch the ship's arrival.

JC noted, "This is a pretty long and narrow canal. It must have been a squeeze for the cargo ships back in the old days."

Susan gave him a glance, "Sweetheart, the Great Lakes have a lot of ports. This is only one. How do you think people moved stuff around in the old days? You should see what comes and goes at Duluth. You're looking at the heartland of America. You Californians don't really have a good handle on history. That's why we're on this trip – well, one of the reasons. Wait till we get onto the Erie Canal." She gave his arm a squeeze.

It wasn't long before the ship was tied up at a dock that gave them a view right down the main street. By this time all the passengers were out lining the rails to have a look. Down on the dock stood a group of local citizens all dressed in 1890's outfits. The men had tight-legged trousers held up by colorful wide suspenders and were wearing straw boaters. The women had on full ankle-length cotton dresses and had donned bonnets. One got the feeling of having just stepped onto the stage of a gay nineties musical film set.

The group was silent and the steam calliope stood on its spindly wheels wheezing slightly but playing no tune. The locals had obviously been informed that there were somber events about to take place. Parked in the street just at the curb behind the greeters was a large cream-colored SUV with darkened windows. The back was open and on the side of the driver's door in discrete but clearly identifiable words was written *Hoyle's Funeral Services*.

The large hatch just below where the Shelbys stood opened as soon as the mooring lines were secure and the simple gangway slid out to the dock. One of the student crew was erecting the safety handrails along the sides of the gangway as two men exited the funeral vehicle and began unloading a gurney from the rear. They made their way through the small group on the dock and up the short gangway into the vessel. They weren't gone more than five minutes before they reappeared, slowly wheeling the gurney down the gangway with its sorry burden. Avery Gunderson's remains were tightly zipped up in a black plastic leatherette body bag. It appeared a very light load for these two well muscled men. It took them less than a minute to reach their van, slide the gurney in, wheels folding as it went, and slamming the back shut.

Susan bent close to JC and whispered, "We never saw the body. I wonder if he was really in that sack."

JC could hardly restrain his laughter. He whispered back, "Who else my sweet could possibly be in the bag. It's got to be Avery."

At that moment the calliope began to tootle off key "Ain't She Sweet" and the group on the shore began to wave. Four men detached themselves from the rest and began voicing the words to this old familiar song in barbershop style.

Susan bounced away from the rail straightening up and exclaiming in a clearly audible voice, "Now this is my idea of a very good funeral. Should we all join in?"

JC threw up his hands in exasperation and turned to go into the lounge. "That gal. She is something. I don't know whether to kiss her or spank her."

About that time the speaker sounded again, somewhat irreverently, "All right folks, all ashore that's going ashore. Be back aboard by five. We sail at six and there are good eats on the docket for supper."

◊

Susan and JC spent the day wandering in and out of the colorful but very touristy shops. It was indeed a charming little town and really had a lot going for it. They had lunch at a soda fountain sitting on wire-backed chairs at a small round marble-topped table. It was a hamburger and malt for each of them.

The museum filled them in on the colorful history of Manistee and they even were able to catch a glimpse of what the thought might be some movie people setting up down a side street for shooting.

At four thirty they made their way back to the dock and arrived just as a sedan pulled up next to the gangway. One of the men they had seen earlier wheeling Avery ashore got out carrying a carton.

"That must be Avery returning after a warm day in Manistee," said Susan.

"Sweetheart, you had better let up on the jokes. Somebody is going to take offence pretty soon if they hear you," grumped her husband.

"JC, I don't think anyone in that group is going to shed many tears. Beside if we keep the same seating we will have one less at the table. That means more elbow room and more fresh bread for the rest of us."

By this time JC had given up responding and just forged ahead to the gangplank with Susan still grinning trailing behind.

◊

Dinner was served as soon as they were underway and headed north out on Lake Michigan. The table occupancy had shrunk to five and the atmosphere was just a little negative in mute recognition of the absence of the missing head of the Gunderson expedition. Dinner tonight was chicken and dumplings, a favorite of JC's, so he at least was in a pretty good mood. He only hoped secretly that Susan would stifle herself and not come out with some smart crack about Avery Gunderson missing a good meal. One particular blessing was that no member of the clan had decided to bring the ashes up to the dining area for display.

They had all been served coffee and were beginning to relax from a really good meal when Captain Jack made a surprise appearance at the forward end of the dining area. So far on this voyage he had not been much in evidence to the guests.

One of the passengers quipped, "Who's steering the boat, Cap?"

He smiled and waved to the fellow, "Don't worry, Bob is a licensed and fully qualified ship's master. He's giving me a break.

"I wanted to fill you in on tomorrow's program. When you wake up we will be approaching the Mackinac Bridge. You won't want to miss this. For a lot of you from other parts of the country you may not have even heard of it. It is one of the major suspension bridges of the continent and is a spectacular sight. We'll be passing under it on our way to Mackinac Island. By the way, when you see it spelled it doesn't look like it sounds. It's from an Indian word – I can't ever remember what that is – and is pronounced 'Mack – in – awe' not 'Mack – in – nack.'

"Back in the 1800s when the Brooklyn Bridge was built people here began to think along the lines of getting a better way to travel between upper and lower Michigan. In the twenties ferries were introduced to take care of the heavy tourist traffic during the popular summer months. It got so busy that even with nine ferries the backup along the highway waiting to get over could stretch as far as sixteen miles. Then in the fifties, after a lot of politics and wrangling, the bridge was completed. The total structure including the approaches is over five miles long and the span itself is the longest suspension span from anchor to anchor of any in the country.

"When we pass through the Mackinac Straits at the bridge we will be in Lake Huron. Just a few miles further on we come to our day's stop at Mackinac Island. This little island figured pretty big during the war of 1812. Two battles were fought against the British there. Today there are about 500 permanent residents and the island is designated a national preserve. There is a small airport for some of the more moneyed visitors to use to get to their summer homes. The entire shoreline is only eight miles long. No motorized vehicles are allowed on the island. The little village is very colorful. The streets are filled with horse drawn tourist buses, bicycles, walkers and even roller skates. The buildings and architecture are beautiful and the flower gardens a glory to behold. Down at the dock you will probably see goods stacked that have been delivered by boat waiting for horse drawn drays to take them to their various destinations. Some say that there are more horses here than permanent residents."

With that, Captain Jack paused and waited for questions. He was quite a contrast to Bob Walden, his first mate, with his slight build and very neatly trimmed beard and moustache. He had pale complexion that made a sharp contrast to his jet-black hair and facial adornment. He couldn't have weighed in above 130 pounds, but gave the impression of a tightly contained and competent individual up to any contingency. He was not given to extraneous talk but seemed ready for efficient and instant action if the occasion demanded. This certainly instilled confidence in his traveling companions. It was a necessary personal trait given that there were only two skilled seamen aboard, not counting the cook and the summer college students.

Jonathon Gunderson smiled at the conclusion of the captain's spiel and addressed the table in general, "It looks like clear sailing from here on. You know, being a Chicagoan you would think this would all be old hat for me, but it's not. I think Myrtle and I have been so wrapped up in my work over the years that we really never knew what was right in our back yard."

The mood was lightened and everyone at the table began to chatter and trade comments about the next day's adventures and what might be waiting further down the line.

Susan leaned close to JC and whispered out of the side of her mouth, "Old Avery – soon forgotten and everyone a couple of mil richer."

"Be quiet, Susan!"

CHAPTER 5 –
MACKINAC ISLAND

The entire company of guests aboard the little *Chicago Belle* was gathered on the sun deck above the dining and lounge area at seven-thirty the next morning. No one intended missing the beautiful Mackinac Bridge. A gentleman standing next to the Shelbys at the forward deck rail was waxing enthusiastic and explaining everything to whomever was within earshot.

"The governor of Michigan has a house there, you know? They don't allow pedestrians or bikes on the bridge." He bubbled on; "Each year in the spring they open the bridge for one day for the annual walk-across. The governor leads the way."

It wasn't really annoying. Most didn't really know anything about this part of the world. It was indeed a remarkable sight; especially for this part of the world which had a feeling of remote wilderness about it. Probably ninety percent of the citizens of the United States had never heard of the structure.

JC marveled, "I've seen the Golden Gate a million times and the Oakland Bay but this is really something. I would never have guessed." He gave Susan a squeeze and asked, "Have you seen it before?"

She said, grinning, "No, but I knew about it. Michigan is a neighbor of ours, you know." She gazed up at the span as they approached the stretch of water beneath it, "It's bigger than I imagined and certainly beautiful."

Maude Gunderson appeared at their side as the ship left the bridge behind and said, "This is a real treat for me. Living in Manhattan has its down side."

"How is that?" said Susan.

"Well we surely have our bridges, but also we've got about ten million people using them most of the time. Even living in comparative luxury I get a feeling of being hemmed in." She seemed to be waxing philosophic at the moment. She grasped the rail and looked out over the lake at the distant island they were approaching. "This is truly refreshing." She turned and gave them a smile.

JC asked, "What do you think of the cruise – the idea of the cruise, that is?"

She gave a crooked smile, "You mean the Gunderson Saga? Well, it matters not to me. As I said earlier, I could have done without. I never really knew old Avery or his brothers but I guess it's my duty." Then with a change of tone, "I am really glad for the others. They could use the money." She lapsed into silence for several minutes then said, "I wonder what's at the end. Do you suppose they have some legal beagle waiting at the dock in Rhode Island? Damnedest peculiar business I have ever heard of."

Hoping to raise the mood to a happier level Susan said, "Maude, what are your plans for the day on the Island. I hear we have the entire day for touring around. They have some horse-drawn tour buses I hear."

"I have no plans. I actually would like to get away from the bunch for the day if possible," she said.

"Join us. We can make it a threesome. I understand it's a gorgeous town with lots of gardens and turn of the century houses. We can walk or take a bus." Susan gave a little laugh, "No roller skates for me, however, even though they are allowed."

Susan then turned to her husband and with a complete change of subject typical of her, "JC, who do you suppose cleans up after all the horses? What do you suppose they do with all the manure?" she wrinkled her brow. "I'll bet that's why they have such beautiful gardens."

JC and Maude burst out laughing. She could be right.

◊

The ship was docked by nine and all the passengers were making their way by foot, bicycle or horse-drawn bus into the small town and its colorful surroundings. The Shelbys and Maude Snyder had chosen to walk for the first part of their explorations. Maude had suggested they rent a small horse-drawn carriage later for a broader view of the small island. JC had vigorously protested that the expense would be exorbitant but Maude prevailed by pointing out that she didn't have much use for a lot of extra money and it would be her pleasure. Susan didn't say anything but she thought it was a capital idea. Her hip still gave her a twinge or two at times.

The main street of the village, which was really most of it, was lined with colorful small shops and a few homes. Nearly all of the construction was painted white and of wood, and most of the homes, called 'cottages' were well off the ground on high foundations and seemed to be of two stories with an attic floor above those. They struck the Shelbys as small castles with their turreted roofs rather than cottages. The entire town seemed frozen in time at a period of about 1910. A brochure about the town that they had picked up at a stand on the pier stated the permanent winter population was about four hundred and fifty with an increase in the summer by regular summer residents and tourist visitors to several thousand.

It was a busy and bustling place. They were passed by the clattering hooves of horse-drawn vehicles and bell-dinging bicycles as they made their way up the few blocks of the main street. Maude suggested they look in at the small museum and then plan where they might like lunch. One possibility was to hire a carriage and go up to the Grand Hotel. They had heard of its reputation and had decided it was worth a special visit.

It was only eleven, though, and Susan insisted she wanted to give the gardens a better look. Flowers seemed to be the main feature of nearly all the homes on the island. During the relatively short summer season the entire place was awash with color. Having grown up in Chicago she had not had the privilege of that much color. Surely, Chicago did have flowers, but not like these.

While they wandered slowly from garden to garden Susan said, "Tell me something about your life in New York, Maude. It must be very exciting. More than Chicago life, I bet."

Maude frowned slightly, "Susan, I had a wonderful husband. Oh dear! How I do miss him. He was in the financial business. I never really understood what he did but then..." she fell silent for several moments. "He died quite unexpectedly." She heaved a little sigh. "Maybe if we had had a little more relaxation; taken a few vacations; hiked the Grand Canyon. Maybe he would have survived a little longer. I really do miss him. He had a lot of fine qualities." Then she brightened up, threw her shoulders back and said, "He left me a rich widow. I have to give him that. We just have to go on, don't we?"

JC asked, "Maude how about this Gunderson business? Did you really have to participate?"

"Yes. I told you before. It's for the sake of the others."

Susan said, "But then there is Abe?"

Maude said, "Yes, then there is Abe. No one has ever met him; at least no one in this bunch, except maybe Ed. He lives in Tempe, Arizona. Avery said when we first gathered that a judge had issued an order based on Abe's illness that exempted him from the arrangement."

Changing the subject, Susan asked, "Tell us a little about the Darlings."

"What's to tell?" snapped Maude. "They live in or about Hollywood, and as far as I can tell, have no prospects... or talent, whatsoever." She gave a smile, "I shouldn't be so judgmental. I don't really know them at all. This is the first time I have ever encountered them."

JC said, "Jonathon and Myrtle seem a nice couple. Do they have any children?"

Maude said, "Not that I know of. I like them. They are both pretty solid citizens. Maybe I'm partial to the big city folks."

JC continued, "All of this seems a far cry from a large farming operation in North Dakota."

"Doesn't it though?" replied Maude without further comment.

◊

The carriage they hired to take them up to the Grand Hotel was part of a package tour of this magnificent structure. It included the gourmet buffet lunch and a tour of the hotel itself. The Grand Hotel was billed as having the longest front porch in the world, and so it seemed. Neither Maude nor certainly not the Shelbys had ever seen anything quite so impressive. It was set on high ground surrounded by lush growth and with a view of Lake Huron that seemed to extend forever on clear days. Today was such a day. It was hard to believe that this kind of magnificence could be built and maintained in this environment, limited as it was to the warm season. JC wondered what they did in the dead of winter. The snowfall must be serious at times.

Their visit to the hotel occupied the remainder of the day. There was no time to tour the rest of the island, small as it was. Their carriage took them back to the pier late in the afternoon. Bob had announced a boarding time of five PM and leaving at five-thirty.

Most of the passengers crowded the sun deck as they sailed away to bask in the warmth of the low summer sun and to get a final view of what would probably be the most picturesque of their many stops on this tour. The sad beginning of the trip seemed to be forgotten by most.

CHAPTER 6 –
LAKE HURON

C aptain Jack came into the dining area to greet them all at dinner as they sailed away from Mackinac Island. "I hope you all had a good time at that beautiful vacation spot. It is certainly one of the treasures of the Great Lakes region.

"We have about four hundred and fifty miles to go before our next stop. It will take us over two days. Lake Huron is one of the big ones. At the southern most point of Huron we enter a long canal that takes us into Lake St. Claire, then more canal past Detroit. We won't be stopping in Detroit but will anchor early just past Detroit near the Ford Museum. We have a bus ready there to get you to the museum and back. It would be criminal to sail right past. It is one of the great science and tech museums of this country. Ford wanted to display a sample of every piece of technology and machinery ever produced in this country. I believe he more than succeeded.

"If the weather holds, and I think it will, you be able to lounge on the upper deck or relax in the shade available on the after deck." He smiled and looked at one of the couples. "I know you two are scrabble fiends. Tomorrow is your chance to show your stuff in the lounge." Everyone tittered.

Susan whispered, "They can skip me. I ain't no good at spelling."
JC laughed and gave her a squeeze, "That makes two of us."

◊

The trip south down the length of Lake Huron was to take two days. The morning of the first day dawned cloudy. Bob came on the speaker announcing a small rain shower in the offing.

"We will be blessed with clearing skies about noon. The crew from Brown will be rigging the rails and setting up the lounges and tables on the upper sun deck right after lunch. Weather reports show that we should have clear sailing for the rest of the day and through tomorrow."

JC and Susan spent the morning reading and assiduously avoiding the scrabble experts without appearing rude. Someone had turned the TV on to a morning cooking show. Once on and tuned in no one seemed to have the courage to change the channel. The seating in the lounge area was crowded with the light rain shower driving nearly everyone inside. A few brave souls were entrenched on the aft deck under the overhanging shelter of the upper sun deck and managing to stay dry and more or less quietly alone with their books and magazines.

After lunch the weather did clear and the sun came out. JC and Susan cold hear the rattle of furniture being set up on over their heads and decided to join the exodus from the dining and lounge area to the deck above. Several of the guests headed to their cabins for a short afternoon nap. It promised to be an uneventful day.

Susan found a lounge chair under an umbrella and settled in with a book she had picked up from the shelf down below. JC saw Ed Gunderson standing alone near the front of the deck leaning on the rail and peering apparently at the lake and sky ahead and decided it might be a good time to get acquainted. Mealtime had not been conducive to serious conversation. The recent tragedy of the senior Gunderson's death seemed to put the quietus on much table talk.

JC joined Ed at the rail and after a few minutes said, "Very sorry about you brother, Mr. Gunderson; quite a shock."

Gunderson turned and gave JC a slight smile, "Yes it was, Mr. Shelby." There was continued silence as both leaned on the rail and continued their inspection of the flat horizon ahead. "Finally Ed Gunderson spoke, "It will take some getting used to, I suppose. I've worked with Avery for a good many years – ever since I left the Army after Vietnam."

JC said, "Please call me JC. Everyone does." Then changing tack, "Do you have a family Mr. Gunderson?"

Ed said, "You better call me Ed. It's the only name I come to – too many Mr. Gundersons around most of the time." Then he continued, "I've lived there on the farm with Avery all these years – never did find the right woman. It's been just Avery and me." He sounded downright depressed. It was hard to tell if he was sad because he had lost Avery or sad because he had been stuck with his older brother all those years.

JC then asked, "How about your other brother Abe, the one that couldn't make it on this trip? Do you see him often?"

Ed grunted, "Haven't seen Abe in five years. Don't hear much from him either. Avery says he hears but I don't. I always liked Abe. Never could figure out why he would go off to Arizona like he did and then never call or write me." He stood back from the rail and gave JC a hard look. "It ain't right. I often thought something was haywire and I tried to get something out of Avery. He never was one to communicate much." He shook his head and looked down at the water over the rail.

JC tried one more tentative probe. "I understand he couldn't come on this trip – had a doctor's excuse or something?"

Ed mumbled, "Yeah, sick, Avery said – don't know what."

Hoping to brighten the mood JC said, "I understand your brother got a really good deal on the farm. What sort of operation did you have?"

Ed perked up a little, "We had about 10,000 acres – most of it in wheat. It was probably the best wheat land in North Dakota. Had a lot of machinery – most of it new – everything up to date. There was a pretty large complex of buildings including a very nice two story house – had a covered porch clear around – barns – the lot. We hired a lot of folks. It was almost like a small town. It was a nice operation and I enjoyed doing the work I did. It sort of compensated for Avery being an old SOB a lot of the time. He made a good deal with ConAgra – couldn't turn it down."

"How was it again that the proceeds of the sale had to be divided among the surviving Gundersons?" asked JC.

"That was the instruction in Pa's will. That was Ezra Gunderson, the fellow that homesteaded and built up this farm. He wanted to make sure that when his boy Avery had done his best with the farm and was ready to retire that everyone would have a share. I understand it's iron clad legally."

"What's the connection to Jonathon?" asked JC.

Ed gave a snort, "We hardly ever met them before. Pa had a younger brother, Samuel. Sam moved out as soon as he was old enough – wanted the city life – went to Chicago. Jonathon is his son. He's my first cousin same as Maude. She's Sam's daughter." He was quiet for a long minute then looking out over the lake again mused, "She did all right - married into Wall Street. I don't begrudge her her share, but she sure doesn't need it."

JC couldn't help but think that this was a pretty complicated arrangement and just a bit weird. He had never heard of anything like it before.

◊

In their cabin before dinner JC filled Susan in on the added details he had gleaned from his conversation with Ed Gunderson.

Susan said, "It's a funny situation to say the least. This guy Ed sounds a bit pathetic. I feel sorry for him. From all I've heard about Avery and from our very brief view of him it couldn't have been much fun living with him for all those years," then taking JC's hands in hers she insisted, "I still am suspicious. Nobody does such kooky things."

"Susan, dear, we really don't know all the crazy things that people are capable of – even sane ones – and this bunch seems sane… at least on the surface." He heaved a sigh and gave her a hug. "No matter how hard you try you aren't going to find a murder this far from land," standing up, "Let's go eat."

Susan followed him out the door and said, "This far from land? You forget the casino guy on the *Alexander Nevsky,* the Russian ship." This gave JC a pause. No, he hadn't forgotten the casino guy on the Russian ship.

CHAPTER 7 –
DEARBORN, MI

Before breakfast the *Chicago Belle* made its way into the narrow waters that threaded their way past Detroit and down to the day's stopping point near the Henry Ford Museum in Dearborn, Michigan. Bob made his usual appearance at breakfast to give them the pitch for the day's activities.

"Too bad we have only a day here. My guess is that one could probably spend a year of days and still not see it all. Henry Ford's museum is enormous. It's an indoor-outdoor affair and can't possibly be explored in one day. The outdoor part is Greenfield Village and depicts, through grounds and buildings, important aspects of the history of this country. You probably won't have time to take that in. the indoor part is twelve acres in size and is packed with everything made by the hands of Americans during our entire history. Ford felt that the way to show what this country is was to show what we have made and used. These items range from Edison's last breath preserved in a sealed test tube to the giant steam locomotive called the *Allegheny* used to haul coal over the Allegheny Mountains. Manufactured in 1941, it weighs in at 600 tons and is the largest railroad engine ever built.

"Many of the exhibits are hands on and interactive. You will be able to play all day. Have a look at Lindbergh's small vacation travel trailer that he used when he was deep in the throes of writing. Then there's the first airplane, a tri-motor, to fly over the South Pole.

"If you had several days you could take the tour of the River Rouge Plant, employing 100,000 people at one time and covering square miles of ground. Inside are 100 miles of railroad tracks. Cars from the Model A on to today's trucks were manufactured here. The scale of this place is beyond imagination.

"The *Chicago Belle* sails at five PM to traverse a little of Lake Erie before we tie up in Cleveland for the night. Some of you might want to sample some of the sights there."

Bob was about to leave the dining salon when he turned around, apparently having an added thought. He gestured to Jonathon at our table and made his way over.

"Mr. Gunderson, do you and your wife like the theatre?

Myrtle smiled, "We certainly do." Then turning to her husband said, "We haven't been to a real play since we went to that dinner theatre down on Michigan Avenue."

Bob held out two pieces of cardboard, "Here are a couple of tickets to a small theatre in Cleveland. I hear they are very good. They have only about 100 seats but they have an excellent reputation." He looked down at the tickets. "Ah, I see they are performing *A Delicate Balance*." He looked up. "Have you seen that before? It's an old classic."

Myrtle responded quickly, "Oh yes. It's wonderful. I saw it years ago. I think it's by Edward Albee and originally starred Hume Cronyn and Jessica Tandy." She looked at her husband. "Let's go dear. We live so near and yet have never actually been there."

Jonathan chuckled, "Well, okay. But I don't think we've missed much by not having seen Cleveland."

Bob said, "We tie up right downtown and the theatre is only a few blocks from where we'll be. You can walk or take a cab if you like. It shouldn't be very expensive." He looked down at the tickets.

I see the play begins at eight. We've got plenty of time. We should be there by seven at the latest." He then handed over the tickets.

◊

It was a glorious day. The Shelbys shared an opinion with all the rest of the passengers – this place was amazing. There was nothing else like it in America or any place else as far as they knew. What was even more amazing to them was how little seemed to be generally known about this fabulous museum across the country. JC said he had never heard of it and Susan, even from next door in Chicago, hadn't either. Chicago had its Museum of Science and Industry, and it certainly was well known, but it couldn't' compare to the Henry Ford establishment.

At dinner that evening as the ship made its way across the end of Lake Erie the table talk was all about the wonders everyone had seen that day. There was so much to see that everyone seemed to have a different story to tell.

Jonathon and Myrtle excused themselves before dessert and coffee to dress for their theatre evening.

As they left the dining lounge Jonathon was saying, "Dear, we don't have to dress. It's just a small theatre."

"All the more reason, Jonathon. We'll be more of a stand out in a small crowd. I want to fit in."

He shook his head ruefully as he went the door and muttered, "We would not be a stand out... anywhere."

Susan and JC quickly finished their dinner and went out on deck to watch as the ship approached the Cleveland waterfront. It was just sundown and lights were coming on in the tall buildings lining the shore. They were preparing to dock at the Erie Street Pier, the center of Cleveland's newly developed urban shore.

CHAPTER 8 – CLEVELAND, OH

The Shelbys stood at the rail just outside their cabin and watched as the ship tied up to the brightly lit dock. Behind the dock the blazed the lights of a large modern city, newly revitalized.

"Susan, do you want to go ashore and take in the sights?"

"Thanks, JC, but we have really had a big day. As far as I'm concerned this cruise is for resting not wheeling around a big city. I've got my own big city back on the other side of Lake Michigan." She hugged him. "Why don't we just have an early night of it and go to bed?" She gave him a sly look, "It might be more entertaining."

JC was more than willing. They stayed at the rail for another thirty minutes and watched as a small gaggle of guests straggled off the ship for their evening on the town. At the bottom of the gangplank they spotted the Gunderson couple just setting foot ashore. The two of them turned and gave them a wave. JC shouted out.

"Enjoy yourselves. Tell us about the show tomorrow at breakfast."

◊

Susan groggily opened her eyes and stared at the blank wall next to their bunk. The first thought that entered her mind was that something peculiar was going on. She was aware of the cacophony of city sounds in the background. That was not what was bothering her. It was the light on the wall. It was reddish and it wavered and flickered. Slowly she began to hear the sounds of sirens. That was not strange. One heard sirens in the big city all the time. She couldn't' figure out why the sound bothered her tonight. JC had always said she had great powers of intuition. Maybe that was what was kicking in.

As she lay there she kept turning over in her mind the peculiarities that they had both garnered about their travelling companions, the Gundersons. Half asleep she wondered if flickering lights, sirens and Gundersons might somehow be connected. That, of course, was pure nonsense. They couldn't possibly be. JC had often accused her of being overly obsessive. Her obsession about crime had turned out to be a pretty good thing in the past. They wouldn't have had a career in the sleuthing business without it.

One last thought entered her mind. They were on a ship. Accidents aboard ships are serious matters. She had learned that, much to her distress and acute physical pain, aboard the Russian cruise ship. It was not wise to lie about and think while something disastrous might be in the offing. She sat up abruptly and shook JC roughly.

"JC, wake up. Something is happening. We need to get up and see what's going on."

JC knew better than to try to avoid the call. He sat up.

"What's up, sweetheart?"

"Who knows?" she answered getting out of bed and starting to dress. She had to get just a little decent before appearing out on deck. The passageway their cabin opened out onto on the starboard side of the ship was brightly lit by the pier lights. It was almost like being on stage to stand just outside their door.

In half a minute JC joined her at the rail and joined her in scanning the city scene before them.

"I don't see much." He said. "There appears to be a fire over there." He pointed. "It's probably about three or four blocks away."

As they watched the fiery glow died away and the sights and sounds of Cleveland at night returned to normal.

Somewhat abashed, Susan said, "I'm sorry. I shouldn't feel jumpy. I don't know why I feel like something is about to happen." She looked quite contrite. "Having that old man die on us the second day isn't any good reason. I know. Let's go into the lounge and have some iced tea or lemonade or something. I don't want to go back to bed right away."

It was ten-thirty and the lounge was nearly deserted. They found a couch against the back wall and sat in silence sipping their drinks. They hadn't been seated more than fifteen minutes when they heard voices at the foot of the gangway on the pier. JC got up and had a quick look from the deck outside.

He came back in quickly and said, "Susan, you may have been on to something. It's a fire department car and a police car. I think I spotted Captain Jack talking to a couple of the officers."

Susan got up and had a look too. "I think they're coming on board. Captain Jack is herding them up the gangway."

A few moments later someone on the deck outside the door said, "Captain, have you got a place we can sit and talk for a few minutes?'

The captain apparently indicated they were all to come into the lounge. JC and Susan didn't move. They quietly kept their seats on the couch while the newcomers gathered at one of the dining tables with the captain.

The captain asked, "What happened officer? We had a couple of our passengers out there tonight. Are they okay?"

The lieutenant from the fire department took over the explanation. The accompanying police officer held his silence for the moment. "There was a fire in a small downtown theatre. I'm afraid there were some serious injuries and may also have been a couple of fatalities. We haven't made complete identifications yet but two of the patrons were apparently trapped in the small balcony of this little theatre and were overcome by smoke. The fire was pretty bad and we got it out in a hurry but had trouble accessing the balcony. The door was jammed. Our men had to wear smoke gear in order to break in. It was really bad up there. There were just two persons in the space and they were in a very bad way. Smoke rises you know and they certainly got the worst of it. We're investigating at the moment to try and find out why they were unable to get out with most of the other patrons."

At that moment the police officer seemed to get a call on his portable radio. He held up his hand to signal silence and listened intently to the barely audible squawking coming from his hand set. When it was done he turned to the pair and said, "That was word from the unit at the theatre. The injured have been taken off to the hospital and one unit is still on the scene. They say that the two that were in the balcony have died – smoke inhalation it seems. Papers in their wallets have identified them as Jonathon and Myrtle Gunderson."

Susan gave a squeak of horror, causing every face to turn to where they were seated.

"Were they special friends of yours?" asked the police officer turning to them.

JC replied quickly, "Well, yes. We have only just met them but they were our table companions and they were from Chicago like my wife Susan here. We are just devastated to hear this news. We quite liked them and thought of them as friends."

Susan had started to cry now. Captain Jack got up from the table and came over to sit down by her. He tried to give her a little comforting pat. This was obviously a rare occurrence in his boating experience and he really didn't know quite what to do.

He then turned to the two officials and said, "What are we supposed to do at this point? I've got a ship full of guests expecting to take an exciting vacation cruise. We've got a long ways to go."

The fire lieutenant hesitated for quite some time then said, "This is really outside our experience. I'm not sure what we can or will do. I appreciate your point about moving on, even in the face of this terrible tragedy. On the other hand we have some investigating to do. I'm just trying to work out in my mind how to proceed.

"Do I understand that there are others of that family aboard?" the fire lieutenant asked.

Captain Jack nodded. "Yes, there are four others of the same family. They are not closely connected. They come from different places. This cruise is a sort of family reunion I understand."

JC gave a sardonic snicker under his breath.

The captain hesitated for a long minute, then with a touch of reluctance added, "The patriarch of the group, a Mr. Avery Gunderson, died of a massive heart attack on our second day out. His remains were handled in Manistee and the group insisted we continue our journey."

Both the policeman's and the fireman's eyebrows went up a notch at this news. Fire lieutenant then said, "At the very least we suggest you will stay with us here for part of tomorrow while we continue our investigation into the cause of the fire and the police will at that time have a chance to talk to the remaining relatives – and anyone else who has something relevant to tell us."

Changing the subject he asked, "Who else went ashore this evening – any of your crew for example – other passengers? Is everyone back on board at this moment?"

Captain Jack replied, "One of my younger crew is posted on the deck below. His name is -"he blushed slightly, "that is, he is familiarly called Up Chuck. He is to keep an accurate log of who goes ashore and who comes aboard. We can't sail till everyone is accounted for."

"Please ask him to join us here for a moment," said the police officer.

The captain stepped out onto the deck and called down over the railing to the open door below for the young student to join them in the lounge for a minute. Up Chuck appeared at the forward door within seconds. The police officer asked him to be seated at the table and then briefly filled him in on what had happened. The young man blanched at the news.

"Now sir," said the officer, "We need to know who went ashore and whether they have all returned. Please give us a run down."

Up Chuck had a clipboard in his hand. He glanced down at it and said, "Everyone, sir. They're all back aboard – except, of course, the Gundersons." At that he moaned slightly and looked like he might break into tears.

"What about other crew members? Did any of them go ashore while you were on duty?"

"No sir. Bob, the first mate, had me helping him get some supplies up to the kitchen while we were tying up. I didn't take over the gangway until everything was secure and we were ready to let folks go off. Actually, sir, only about six people went ashore. None of the crew set foot off the ship."

The officer noted the names of the other four passengers. They would participate in a question and answer session in the morning, then asked again, "Did either the captain or the first mate or any other crew person leave the ship at any time?"

The student was quite earnest, "No sir, it is just as I said."

The two officers stood up. The policeman said, "I am posting a man at the foot of the gangway for the night. We see it as a bit odd that those poor people couldn't seem to get out of that balcony. By tomorrow we'll have more information. We aren't saying there was any funny business, but we have to have an excess of caution in situations we don't quite understand. With that the two of them smiled and thanked the captain and the others present and took their leave."

Susan tugged at JC's sleeve and whispered, "Let's go up on the sun deck for a while. We need to talk."

The deck was deserted. Either the rest of the guests were asleep in their quarters or were in the lounges all abuzz with the terrible news.

They found a corner up near the pilothouse that seemed well protected from the evening breeze as well as any accidental ears.

"JC, I think you will admit that we are pretty close to having a major crime on our hands."

JC said, "We really don't know yet what happened at the theatre. It could truly have been an accident."

"Sure," said Susan, "forty million dollar accident." She was frustrated. "Look, it's not an accident. It's murder. And there could be more. Don't forget that there are still four Gundersons left."

"Five including Mr. Darling. Don't forget Abe. Come on, dear. Are you actually suggesting that one of those people could be a mass murderer?" He shrugged his shoulders and splayed his hands in frustration.

"You bet," she said. "We have a chore to do. There is plenty of motive about. All we have to figure out is means." She became more practical. "Tomorrow you're going to have a talk with the police and fill them in on our background. I think we can really help. We know all those people. We are probably closer to them than anyone else."

JC rubbed his chin; "You are certainly right about that. From my talk with Ed we may be closer to them than even some of their friends back home. I got the feeling that they lived a pretty isolated life, Ed and Avery I mean."

Susan was quiet for quite a few minutes then a little pensively as she looked out over the city, "It's hard to see poor dear Maude as a murderer but we should have learned better, haven't we? If murder sits in someone's soul it can be invisible and actually fester there for years unnoticed. We have no idea how long resentments might have built up."

JC knew that Susan's ideas usually bore fruit, and even though he felt they should butt out he reluctantly agreed. "So what do you want me to do? There's nothing can be done tonight, obviously."

"No, not tonight," she said. "Tomorrow morning I think it would be a very good idea for you to go into the city with the police and talked to someone up the line and ask them to check us out. Maybe we could get something of an assignment out of this. I have a strong feeling that the ship will be given the green light to sail some time tomorrow, and wouldn't it be nice if we could be aboard as secret agents working to ferret out the monster that perpetrated this business?"

◊

After breakfast the next day JC hung around in the back of the lounge while two detectives questioned the four passengers that had been ashore the night before. Captain Jack had asked to sit in.

When the questioning seemed to be finished he spoke up, "Detective, have you any idea when we might be released? I really feel we need to try and keep as much to schedule as possible. I've called the owner in Rhode Island and he is most willing to cooperate, naturally, but urged me to ask for permission to sail on."

The detective was sympathetic. "Sir, we expect to have the matter cleared up as far as you are concerned by noon. I think you could plan on that."

The captain was visibly relieved. He excused himself and headed for the forward door leading to the control bridge and his quarters.

As he left he said, "Thank you. I will see to the arrangements. I must let Bob and the others know."

As the two detectives started to leave JC stepped forward, "Pardon me. Could I have a word before you go?" Then added, "Down on the pier if you don't mind."

The detective lieutenant looked a bit puzzled but answered, "Of course, let's go."

The three of them filed down the inside ladder to the door onto the gangway. Once outside the detective turned to JC, "What have you got for us?"

JC looked around to be sure they were not near anyone and said, "Sir, my wife, Susan, and I believe we have some useful information about this situation. I would request I accompany you back to police headquarters. It's not something we can discuss here on the pier and it might be vital to understanding what occurred last night at that theatre."

The officer looked puzzled but couldn't refuse a reasonable request. After all, they really hadn't the answers to what may have happened in that fire yet. He assented and escorted JC to the waiting police vehicle.

At police headquarters JC was ushered into a large and rather well furnished office. The man at the desk stood and greeted him.

"I'm Chief Mackey. You are Mr. Jeremiah Shelby I understand, one of the passengers on the *Chicago Belle*. Please sit down." He waved JC to a seat and then took a seat himself. "What have you for us?"

JC began, "Chief, most call me JC and I am actually out of uniform at the moment, but I am on active duty with the US Navy, a lieutenant. While on official duty in the armed forces I have been involved in several crime investigations. I am not at liberty to go into details on these matters but I can give you some contact information with the intelligence community in Washington as verification. I have a suggestion – a simple request actually.

"After you have vetted my credentials I would like to be allowed to do a little investigation of my own. My wife will assist me. She has been extremely useful in past cases. It would be useful if I had clearance to contact your office by phone when necessary. In addition I don't think it would go amiss to bring in the FBI about now. Perhaps you could make arrangements. The way I see it, this is a multi-state affair. Mr. Avery Gunderson died in waters off the Michigan coast. His remains were cremated at Manistee. It was considered natural at the time but who knows? There is a great deal of money involved."

The chief frowned, "The FBI? This was a very unfortunate accident here in Cleveland, was it not? Do you have reason to believe otherwise?"

"Chief, I think there is more to it than that."

He then proceeded to fill the police chief in on the situation with the Gundersons and the possible money motive.

The chief mulled this over for a few moments then scribbled a note. He rang a buzzer and an officer came into the room. He handed him the note.

"Please try to get a hold of Admiral Wilkerson at Naval Intelligence in Suitland, Washington; when you have him on the line transfer the call in here. Thank you."

Then he turned back to JC. "We will see how that goes in a few minutes. Meanwhile let me fill you in on what we have found out about the fire. I am confident that what you are telling me is true."

"Thank you, Chief."

"This very small legitimate theatre used to be a movie house in the old days. A few years back they gave up trying to attract patrons to their silent films. They showed only old classics. I understand there are about one hundred seats. Most are on the main floor but there are twelve in a small balcony. These balcony seats are jammed in next to the old projection booth – two rows – six in each row. The staircase from the lobby leads up on the right and opens into a narrow short hall behind the booth leading to the area behind to the seats.

"Hundreds of old films were stored in the booth. They had been there for a very long time. The space was used for nothing else. Our preliminary investigation shows that a short circuit occurred in some stage lighting wiring that ran through the booth. Unfortunately many of these old films were of the highly flammable acetate type, long out of use these days. The place went up like a bomb.

"The flames quickly engulfed the roof of the building and trapped the only two people in those seats, the Gunderson couple.

The fumes were intense. The people on the main floor were luckier. The fire and smoke were up near the ceiling and they were able to get out with only minor injuries.

"The fire was extinguished fairly rapidly but the roof was a total loss. Although the bodies of the Gundersons showed few burns they were very quickly overcome by smoke and fumes from the burning film."

JC asked, "Chief, that wiring – did it go to lights that were being used during the play? Were those same lights used throughout the play or just near the end?"

"Curious you should ask that, JC. Have you seen the play?" The chief's memory of the play had obviously sparked a connection in his mind to what might have started this conflagration.

JC admitted that he had not and that he was unfamiliar with the story.

The chief laughed bitterly, "What irony! In the last scene the morning sun rises outside the living room where all the action takes place and brilliantly illuminates the garden as seen through the double garden doors. Agnes, the lead, originally played by Jessica Tandy, throws these open as she delivers the final lines of the play. That's when the fire burst out. It must have been that intense white flood used to illuminate the off-stage garden area. It hadn't been used earlier. All the preceding scenes were somewhat dark and gloomy. The garden portion of the set was not involved in the preceding part of the play."

The phone rang on the chief's desk. From his response to the caller it was clearly an answer to his request to Washington. Information was exchanged and the brief call was terminated. As the chief hung up he turned to JC.

"I actually had Admiral Wilkerson on the phone. He has great things to say about you and your pretty wife. I don't think we have a problem here. I will have a word with your Captain Waite and alert him to your status."

JC frowned, "Chief, things will work better for both of us if you kept this business between just us Shelbys and the captain. Others may eventually find out that I am aboard in some official capacity but there is no sense in letting it be known too early."

Mackey readily agreed.

Then JC said, "There is one more thing; just on the off chance that we have a serial crime here. My wife, who has a pretty good instinct for these matters, still wonders about the first death, the old man. When we get to Buffalo I would like to check in with an FBI office. Do you have any connections there?"

Chief Mackey gave a broad grin. "Indeed I do. I'm going to put you in touch with agent O'Kelley, Siobhan O'Kelley." He bent down to the desk and grabbed a pen. "Let me write that out for you. If you don't know the Irish names you'll never figure it out. It sounds like 'Shi–vawn' – it's Irish for Joan - but spelled S-i-o-b-h-a-n."

He stood and escorted JC to the door. With a friendly hand on his shoulder he said, "I will phone Buffalo as soon as you leave." Smiling broadly, "I hope it won't come to that but if it does you'll like working with Agent O'Kelley."

◊

The ship got underway at one o'clock. Most of the passengers were relieved in a way to be leaving Cleveland. Not that it wasn't a good place to visit, but there hadn't been much to do there, and with the awful tragedy that had occurred, most simply wanted to put it behind them and get on with their vacation adventures.

With the police investigation and all the confusion attendant on the tragic fire and loss of the two passengers lunch had been delayed. As the ship left the Cleveland skyline to the west most had settled in around their tables to eat. Sandwiches and salad had been laid out on the buffet table at the head of the dining salon. What had been the Gunderson table was reorganizing itself. Maybe it was an unconscious desire to huddle for protection that prompted the remaining members of the clan to congregate more closely, irrespective of the fact that they really hardly knew each other. The young Darlings had decided to move from where they had normally sat to the table where the Shelbys had settled from the beginning. The group was now back up to six – The Darlings, Maude, Ed, and the Shelbys.

During the meal the ever jolly and irrepressible first mate, Bob Walden, made his usual entrance near the end of the meal for announcements.

"Dear Guests, I must apologize for the delay in getting away from Cleveland, but Captain Jack assures me that it won't affect the schedule seriously. For the rest of this day and tonight we will be making our way down the length of Lake Erie to Buffalo. Buffalo is another one of our major North Eastern cities and represents our first touch with the State of New York. It is also at the head of the Niagara River that connects Lake Erie with Lake Ontario.

Lake Erie is a curiosity in a way. It is very shallow. Ships have to follow a very particular course to avoid going aground. There is a channel down the middle that is maintained for the length of the lake that permits the kind of heavy traffic typical of lake shipping. I'm not saying you could wade across the lake. It is a trifle more than six feet deep. If you couldn't swim you would most likely drown.

"This will be another good day to lounge on the sun deck. I have made sure that Up, Lucy, and Fender are on hand to tend to your needs during the afternoon. We telephoned the owner of the *Chicago Belle* and he agreed that in light of the two unfortunate occurrences among the guests that all libations and refreshments from now on will be on the house."

The brought a few smiles and murmurs of pleasure from the passengers.

Bob continued, "Buffalo will be our stop for tomorrow. We will anchor immediately next to the magnificent water park situated there. This is the site of three navy museum ships: the cruiser, *USS Little Rock*; the destroyer bearing the famous brothers' name, the *USS Sullivans*; and the Submarine, *USS Croaker*. They will all be within a short walking distance from where we tie up.

"The cruise takes a departure from its usual schedule at this point. Obviously we can't take the ship over the Falls. Some of you may have wondered how we get around the problem. It's quite simple really; we take advantage of a canal kindly built by the Canadians for all who travel by water. The Welland Canal goes around the Falls on a twenty-five mile run, complete with its own locks. An interesting stat: 40,000,000 tons of cargo pass through this canal each year. If you stayed with the ship you wouldn't have the pleasure of seeing the Falls. We have engaged two small busses that will carry you all from Buffalo to all of the day's sights and activities and then to the ship anchored on the other side ready to continue on its way down Lake Ontario. It will be a fun day. We've plenty of time to see the sights and take a ride on the *Maid of the Mist* under the Falls."

◊

After lunch JC and Susan found a couple of secluded folding chaises on the sun deck. Looking back they could barely discern the presence of one of America's large cities, Cleveland; looking a head, nothing. Buffalo was yet a long way off.

Susan opened the conversation. "JC give me the dope on your visit with the Chief of Police. We haven't had a chance to talk." She gave him a smile. They hadn't had any privacy since his return from the Police Headquarters, and she could hardly contain herself.

JC knew he might be in trouble at this spot. "Yeah, we had a good talk. Uh – I suggested we might like to have a contact with the FBI in case these deaths were connected in some way."

Susan raised her eyebrows skeptically, "That sounds reasonable; why the hesitation?"

JC stammered, "Well – uh - he gave me the name of someone to look up in Buffalo. I guess we had better do it."

"Who is that?" queried Susan.

"Agent O'Kelley." Snapped JC.

"Fine," said Susan, "so you're going to see this guy O'Kelley in Buffalo."

"Yeah, but it's not a guy it's Siobhan O'Kelley."

Susan grinned from ear to ear and laughed out loud, "JC, you are a darling. That's why I love you so. So ladies from the Emerald Isle can't be FBI agents? Well I certainly hope they can. I consider this good news. I might have aspired to that job myself if I'd had the chance. I can't think of a better idea than having a smart colleen official to back up whatever we might do."

JC blushed some more and settled back in his lounge chair. He got over that hump pretty easily. When was he ever going to learn? Susan was always smarter than he gave her credit for.

CHAPTER 9 –
BUFFALO, NY

Cruising east on Lake Erie was lazy and uneventful. The afternoon passed with most of the passengers up on the sun deck taking advantage of the smooth sailing and the free booze granted by the cruise line owner. JC and Susan stayed in their little corner under the shelter of an umbrella and discussed the developments of the past few days in low voices. The remaining Gundersons seemed to be in low spirits and were not in evidence topside. Susan guessed they might have succumbed to emotional exhaustion. She couldn't blame them.

"JC, the more the days go by the more I feel we are really into something. What do you think?"

"You are the one with the intuitions, but I would have to agree since Chief Mackey seemed to see fit to put us on to the FBI at our next stop," said JC

Susan lapsed into silence for several minutes then, "Sweetheart, I have an idea for our stop in Buffalo. I understand we don't get in there until midmorning tomorrow. Why don't you renew your naval connections by spending the time prowling around the museum ships while I go into town and talk with Agent O'Kelley?" she gave him an arch look. "You wouldn't be offended would you?"

JC smiled, "No, I wouldn't be offended. I would like to meet her." He hesitated. "If anything develops I'm sure I will see plenty of her eventually." Brightening up a little, "I don't know how they manage things. Do you? Will she be able to come on board if something develops? Do you suppose she would just hand it off to someone else further down the line?"

"Don't ask me," said Susan. "I don't believe we've ever had to deal with the FBI." Then she frowned and said, "Oh yeah, I remember now. We did indeed, with the office in Honolulu. My guess is that if we turn up anything she will come to us."

JC leaned back on his chaise smiling thinking about his day among the moored museum ships and muttered to himself, "Ah ha, back on a cruiser with no danger of sea sickness. That will be a treat." The memory of the awful circumstances that had taken him out of the active Navy as a lowly yeoman came flooding back. It was his rough ride on a cruiser that had done him in. His at-sea experiences since had been relatively benign – well, aside from having one cruise ship blown up and sunk beneath his feet off New Zealand.

◊

It was a quiet evening with nearly everyone in their cabins or watching television at the back of the dining lounge. One couple tried to raise some interest in a game but got no takers. JC and Susan spent a half hour out on deck and decided to turn in. Who could know what the morrow would bring.

◊

The day dawned overcast but with his usual jolly air Bob assured everyone that the weather forecast had no rain in it and all should enjoy their day in Buffalo. He explained that they would have most of the day there and the night as well. On the following morning the ship would depart for the Welland Canal and the passengers would be on their way on buses to see the fabled Falls. It was billed as one of the highlights of the trip.

On his way from the dining room by the aft door Bob stopped by the table seating the Gundersons and Shelbys. He casually spoke to the Darling couple.

"Here is something for you to consider. It's a real honeymoon spot and maybe you two would enjoy this."

He gave them an envelope that seemed to hold a brochure of some sort. Darrell thanked him and took a quick look at the envelope.

"Cloe and I will have a good look at this tonight. I'll let you know tomorrow. Is it expensive?" asked Darrell.

Bob replied, "I'm sure it's not. The people are friends of the owner and offered it as a special perk. I got the message this morning. You two came immediately to mind." He gave them a broad smile and a nod to the rest of the table as he left.

◊

The ship was tied up next to the marine park by ten o'clock and most of the passengers had debarked and scattered to their various destinations for the day depending on their particular interests. A large fraction would spend most of the day walking this remarkable park and touring the three ships. It was a wonder to most that the Navy had managed to place such a large floating force this far from the deep-water blue ocean. It seemed an anomaly, but then the destroyer *Kidd* was anchored at Baton Rouge up the Mississippi, also an unlikely place for a US destroyer.

JC headed out for the *Little Rock,* determined to explore every inch of the ship available to the public. He had a deep-seated sense of inadequacy engendered by the fact that here he was a full navy lieutenant knowing practically nothing about navy vessels. He was sure he couldn't repair that lack with a simple one-day visit but it couldn't hurt. He was glad in a way that Susan had volunteered to take the FBI duty and leave him free to explore the park. He stopped just short of the gangway to the *Little Rock* remembering the cell phone in his pocket. He seldom had occasion to use it but now might be the right time. He punched in the Buffalo FBI number and asked for the desk of Agent O'Kelley. She might be a little taken aback to have a young lady show up when a male navy lieutenant was expected. He spoke briefly with O'Kelley. She assured him that she had both their names and would be glad to see Susan.

◊

Susan took a cab to Number One FBI Plaza in the center of downtown Buffalo. She was just a little amazed to see the facility that dominated the area. Imagine getting your address listed like that. The building took up nearly a whole block and was surrounded on the street side by closely spaced concrete decorative balls. Her first thought was that she would hate to lose control of a vehicle and accidentally crash into one of these. They had the look of being able to do serious damage to a car and they would certainly stop you dead in your tracks. The cab entered the small parking lot near the entrance and let her off in front of the large glass entrance doors. After check in formalities she was escorted up onto the second floor and down a long hall to the office of Agent Siobhan O'Kelley.

Agent O'Kelley greeted her at the door to her office and invited her to be seated in a comfortable chair near the desk. This federal agent was a surprise. Susan was not quite sure what she expected. She had watched in years past the Ballykissangel comedy series on TV about the affairs of the small Irish village in which one of the characters, a veterinarian, bore the name Siobhan. She was a hefty lass who looked capable of handling any sheep or cow that might come her way but this Siobhan was anything but hefty. Agent

O'Kelley was all of five feet tall and couldn't have weighed in at more than one twenty. She had flaming red hair and a very fair freckled skin. Her eyelashes and eyebrows had the pale look of a true red head. Her face was nearly perfectly round – not oval. And one would be tempted to say – 'she had the map of Ireland written all over her face.' She was most definitely <u>not</u> one's image of a typical FBI agent. Because of her petite stature she had developed the habit of staying out from behind her desk when she had visitors. Instead, after her guest had been seated, she parked herself on the front corner of her desk. This gave her an advantage during interviews. It did place her strategically 'above' her visitors. Her apparel for office duty was a very smart tailored light gray pants suit, a white blouse with a fairly large bow at the neck. Susan gave her a quick critical examination and wondered briefly if that trim outfit could possibly conceal the obligatory weapon. She presumed that it somehow did.

"Welcome to Buffalo, Mrs. Shelby. Would you like some coffee?" She waved at the closed door.

Susan replied in the negative, then, "Agent O'Kelley, nearly everyone calls me Susan. You may as well, if that's permitted. My husband is JC." She gave a little laugh, "Right now I imagine he is aboard the *Little Rock* pretending it's at sea and being quite happy it really isn't." She gave the agent an arch look, "He suffers from chronic sea sickness."

O'Kelley laughed, "Some sailor." Then more seriously, "I understand from my phone conversation with Chief Mackey that the two of you have been involved with some pretty serious investigations?"

"That's true," said Susan, "Do you want – "

O'Kelley interrupted, "No, I don't need any history. I called the Navy people in DC and got a pretty good run down on you two. Very impressive, I must say." Then she continued, "Why don't we just deal with the current situation? I understand you both have some concern over some coincidental deaths aboard your cruise ship – the *Chicago Belle*, isn't it?"

Susan launched into her spiel, "Ordinarily, one wouldn't be concerned, but I have learned to follow my intuitions. Since this situation involved a possible motive of about forty million dollars it sort of raised my hackles."

O'Kelley raised her eyebrows, "Hmm! That is a fair sum in some quarters. Go on."

Susan proceeded to fill her in on the details of the three deaths that had occurred. "I don't think Chief Mackey is entirely satisfied with the superficial first explanation of the fire in Cleveland," she continued. Then, "I understand that since all this involves two states so far that the FBI might want to help." She didn't explain the term 'so far', which could have produced doubt that there was even a problem.

Agent O'Kelley gave a puzzled frown, "We might have an interest but at the present time there doesn't seem to be any evidence of a crime. I don't see what we can do to assist. And what is it that you need?"

Susan suddenly felt ill at ease and just a little helpless. Maybe this whole thing was a mistake. She was beginning to feel embarrassed. "I'm sorry. I may have made a mistake in coming here. It's just that I have this hunch that things are just not as they should be. It's hard to explain to an outsider. This Gunderson clan and their epic saga are just a little creepy to me. If I hadn't been involved with so much crime in the past I'm sure I would be ignoring all this. I may be just wasting your time."

"Susan, please don't feel that way," said O'Kelley. "Why don't we say we have a partnership? I'll put you on a priority with my phone service so that if you should call we will be in instant touch. There is nothing I can do at the moment but I will be glad to be part of your sleuthing team as you go along." Then more brightly, "I understand that your ship will skip around the Falls tomorrow and that your passengers will all have a day bussing through the Falls area. It should be a wonderful day. Tour groups like this are nearly always given the whole day. You'll be able to take the *Maid of the Mist* below the Falls and get yourselves thoroughly wet, and there are a dozen other wonderful activities." After a moment she added, "Have you or your husband ever been here before?"

Susan said, "Would you believe? I'm from Chicago and have never been here before," then added, "or even through the Great Lakes." Blushing slightly, "It can sort of be a second honeymoon, "Our first one was in London and was spoiled by a couple of very ugly corpses, one of them in the kitchen of our B&B."

O'Kelley gave a hearty laugh, "Okay then, let's leave it at that. Put me on speed dial on your cell phone and have a good time. I understand that you will be leaving your ship in the morning for the day's activities and rejoining it at the end of the day up in Lake Ontario."

◊

As Susan made her way back to the Navy Park she mulled over in her mind the short visit she had had with the little Irish policewoman. She had a feeling of assurance that she had enlisted a powerful assistant in their pursuit of this tenuous suspicion. From here on the shadow of Siobhan O'Kelley would be a presence by their side, come what may.

◊

JC had had a relaxing day at the waterfront and had toured all three of the ships moored there. It was especially pleasant in that none of them were actually at sea rolling about while he was on board. His visit aboard the *Little Rock* had elicited mostly bad memories of his injury in his earlier life and his long recuperation in the Navy offices in Pearl Harbor. Thank goodness that bit of his life was fading into the dim past. Still, he felt a little uneasy about sporting a Navy commission and not having any real expertise to go with it. His superiors seemed to think his detective prowess was sufficient justification and he would just have to go along with the program. Sometimes he wondered if there could ever be a real promotion. He couldn't imagine how that might take place. He was happy enough to be just a lieutenant but then he couldn't help envisioning that extra half stripe once in awhile that would make him a lieutenant commander.

Before dinner he and Susan sat up on the sun deck with a glass of wine each and debriefed each other on the day's adventures. There really wasn't much to tell and most of the time was spent in just looking at the day – or what was left of it.

CHAPTER 10 –
THE FALLS

After breakfast two minibuses took on board the passengers of the *Chicago Belle* for their day at Niagara Falls. The much reduced Gunderson Clan and the Shelbys found themselves on the same bus. Each bus held about twenty passengers. One of the grad student crewmembers was assigned to each bus, the third student, the captain, the first mate and the cook remained with the ship to assist in getting it through the Welland canal and down to the much lower level of Lake Ontario. It was a bright and sunny day. The mood of everyone seemed lifted by the change of venue and the close proximity of everyone on this small crowded bus.

It was only a short drive from Buffalo to the various stops they would make in the vicinity of the Falls. As expected the Niagara Falls area is crowded with hotels, motels, restaurants, and various shops and amusement centers. The broad extent of the Falls gives ample room for the various overlook areas. These would be bustling with cars and busses and the walkways crowded with sightseers.

The bus transporting the Shelbys and the Gundersons had made only one stop on its way to the first of the overlook parking area. That stop had been Long Road on Grand Island. Here the young Darlings debarked to journey down to Sandy Beach on a special adventure of their own. Mr. Darling, Darrell, had briefly mentioned as they were getting on the bus that Bob had put them onto a special deal at the little community of Sandy Beach. He had said that it was an opportunity they couldn't afford to pass up. Darrell didn't say exactly what it was and neither JC nor Susan was able to talk further with them. The Darlings had found seats at the front of the bus with the Shelbys winding up stuck right at the back. Neither of the Shelbys had given it another thought. The excitement of actually seeing these fabulous Falls first hand commanded everyone's attention and chatter.

The student who accompanied them explained that they would first be looking at the upper end of the Niagara River as it flowed north toward Lake Ontario. The bus stopped at a wide parking area where everyone piled out. There wasn't much to see. The broad river seemed very calm and smooth and there was no sign of the Falls that lay some miles farther along. They clearly were not actually visible from this up-river vantage point. The ship's patrons looked out over the river for awhile then most of them made their way into a nearby souvenir shop to spend a little money on their very first Niagara Falls postcards and small Falls trinkets.

Eventually the bus made its way to the prime viewing area. It was also from here that tourists could go down to the dock for boarding one of the many boats bearing the name *Maid of the Mist* for a short trip right into the spray and thunder at the bottom of the Falls. It was billed as an unparalleled opportunity for photos and a guarantee for getting soaking wet. Of course cheap plastic rain gear was provided to all paying customers. JC and Susan opted to stay at the top and just lean on the rail watching the Falls and the activities of the tour boats below. They were in for a fairly long wait since most of the ship's passengers had decided to go for the spray and mist.

As they leaned on the stone parapet bordering the parking area, half hypnotized by the constant roar of the Falls, Susan stood up straight and moved back from the wall, a puzzled look on her face.

"JC, do you hear something?" she asked. "A siren or something. I hope everything's all right."

JC didn't respond right away. His mind was a million miles away and this place was as busy as any tourist attraction could be. A siren would not necessarily be noticeable. There were thousands of cars and buses everywhere.

Susan persisted, "Listen JC. It's more than one." Then she pointed in the air over the Falls. "Hey, there's a helicopter. I'll bet there is something going on."

Her husband finally gave her some attention. "I think you may be right, sweetheart. I sure hope nobody is trapped on the river somehow." He laughed nervously. "I'm sure that doesn't happen these days. They must have every safeguard in the world to protect people."

Susan said in mock amusement, "Yeah, nobody over the Falls in a barrel these days."

The disturbance continued and the sirens grew louder. At one point a police car screeched rapidly into their off-road park and two officers rushed to the wall that they had just been standing by. Other sirens could still be heard, apparently at various distances to the south. Susan did what she often did in times of stress. Her instincts took over and she unobtrusively moved as close to the two police officers as possible. She knew they had radios and that she might be able to eavesdrop on some official information if she was close enough to get some meaning out of the squawking she could hear coming over their handsets. Both men were too involved watching the roaring rushing water as it poured over the precipice on to the rocks below to notice her presence.

She stood listening for several minutes and then moved quietly away to where JC was standing. He was well aware of what she was up to and was anxious to hear her report.

Very quietly and without actually looking at him she continued to peer out at the Falls and said in a low voice, "Someone in a small boat wandered out too far and go caught in the rapids above the Falls. They're afraid they won't be able to get to them in time. That's what that helicopter is doing up there. They are going to try and get a line down to them."

She then moved slowly back to her earlier position. She surely didn't want to miss out on any new developments. JC kept his gaze glued to Susan. There was nothing to see at the moment at the Falls, but Susan's face would surely signal a change in the situation.

She came back and pointed at a particular spot on the edge of the Falls, "They are not having any luck and they think the boat might actually go over the Falls at that point there – where the rock juts out." Then a moment later, "Maybe they can grab the rock or something. There are two people in the boat. I heard them say it's a small motorboat. I guess the motor isn't working."

By this time the two officers were involved in a spirited conversation in low voices. Nothing could be overheard. Both of them were looking over the edge and pointing from time to time. Finally one of them spoke on the radio and the two lapsed into silence and concentrated their gaze on the edge of the torrent of water. JC surmised they had been assigned the job of spotting the place where the craft would land when it went over. Apparently rescue efforts had failed. One of them dashed back to their vehicle and emerged with a pair of binoculars. He arrived at the wall just as a horrified shout went up from the crowd of at least a hundred that had collected to watch the unfolding tragedy from this particular place. The nose of the boat had appeared at the edge. It had hung there for an instance and then plunged over. JC caught a glimpse of two bodies with arms flailing as they separated themselves from the hull of the boat and disappeared in the boiling white curtain of water. The two policemen stood leaning over the wall, one with binoculars, intently scanning the rocks below for signs of either of the victims or their boat.

Susan turned to JC and said grimly, "You know as well as I. It was the Darlings. We've got a serial murderer on our hands."

JC was aghast, "Susan! How can you say that? We know nothing of the sort."

"Too much coincidence, dear," she replied, "Who else? The Darlings departed the bus to visit someone or something down on the beach. The name of the place was Sandy Beach. What, I ask, would someone do that would be very exciting from a beach in the neighborhood of Niagara Falls? Go fishing? I think not. Go boating," she said with an air of very firm finality. "I will call our friend Siobhan in Buffalo. She will want to hear about this at the earliest."

JC was still stunned but what Susan had said made perfect sense. He guessed it wouldn't hurt. He said with some resignation, "Go ahead give her a call."

◊

Agent Siobhan O'Kelley was indeed interested and gave the Shelby's very specific instructions. She sent a car for them and told them to stand by right where they were. They would be taken to the staging area down stream that the authorities had set up if and when bodies or wreckage were recovered. She would meet them there within the hour.

CHAPTER 11 –
THE HOLE STORY

Their FBI driver whisked them down the river to what appeared to be an abandoned garage and boathouse right on the river's edge. Parked outside were three police vehicles, a Coast Guard van and an unmarked vehicle that JC presumed belonged to Agent O'Kelley.

O'Kelley, dressed now in a jumpsuit and jacket bearing the initials FBI in large print on the back and wearing a long billed dark baseball cap emblazoned with similar initials above the bill, greeted them at the large open door of the building. Her small stature certainly did not diminish her apparent importance among the assembled group. She had an air of command even though she surely was not in command of this particular operation. It was the Coast Guard's job, at least up until the present moment. A lot would depend on what was found and examined in the next few hours. The agent had alerted the Coast Guard and other rescue workers to be especially careful with any thing they found – boat wreckage or bodies. She had said that foul play was not out of the question. That was why she was here.

O'Kelley introduced the Shelbys around the gathered group explaining that JC was with Naval Intelligence and was assisting in the investigation of matters that might have a connection to the Darlings. She did not go into further detail and no one expected more. She asked that the two Shelbys be given full access to the accident investigation and noted that they would all stand by and out of the way of the rescue personnel until material evidence could be brought here. There was no hint as to how long that might be.

JC put in a cell call to Captain Jack on the *Chicago Belle*; which by now must be about half way down the Welland Canal. He explained what had happened and suggested that the ship would just have to wait at the river's mouth in Lake Ontario until the police and FBI gave clearance. Captain Jack was clearly unhappy but had no choice in the matter. He said he would inform the owner in Rhode Island. This would surely put them a full day late and would delay their next cruise date by one, maybe two days.

Agent O'Kelley approached them and said, "It looks like we will be here awhile. The Coast Guard is establishing this location as a command headquarters. Anything found in the river or at the foot of the Falls will be brought here – probably by boat." She gestured toward the river. "There is a dock here, and we have plenty of room to collect the recovered materials inside the building." She then pointed to one of the Coast Guard personnel. "The lieutenant here is setting up the communications system. There will be a loudspeaker in the building and all the traffic will be available to whoever is on site to hear."

JC said, "I take it that it would be best if we just stayed here. There's nothing we can do, I trust?"

O'Kelley smiled, "No, I'm afraid not. There's really nothing for me to do either but your idea that there might be a connection between these deaths is reason enough for me to stay with it."

Susan said, "Agent O'Kelley, we'll be just outside. I need to sit for a while. JC and I can go over some of the things we know. We'll let you know if we come up with anything." She pointed to a bench that sat against the outside wall of the building next to the door. "We can watch the river from here and I guess we'll be able to hear your radio chatter inside okay."

"That's fine," said O'Kelley. "I'll know where you are." With that she disappeared back into the shadows of the garage interior.

The pair settled themselves on the weathered bench and sat watching the swirling water just below for several minutes. Finally Susan said, "Okay dear, so we now have a serial murder case on our hands. Have you got any ideas?" She gave him a serious quizzical look.

JC responded after a few long seconds, "I would say that our good old first mate has tipped his hand several times. The thing that bothers me at the moment is the logic of the business. Where's the motive?"

Susan nodded, "Yeah, and why did he seem to give himself away so easily – giving those brochures or what ever to the Darlings and getting those tickets to the play in Cleveland?"

JC thought about this for several minutes. "You know Susan, I think he felt he had such an iron-clad alibi for the times those accidents happened that it didn't matter. We know he didn't leave the ship the night of the fire and, of course, He's aboard the ship now in the canal miles away." He shook his head and gazed at the ground. "As a suspect he's missing a lot of the essentials – obviously motive and opportunity."

Susan added, "- and means. We really don't know how the fire started, except it was electrical the chief said, and how in the world could he steer that little boat over the Falls from way over in the Welland Canal. My guess is that he is simply not concerned about being accused, even if he did have a hand in it.

"Then," she said, after several seconds of pondering, "maybe there is more than one person involved."

"I hadn't thought of that," said JC. "Do you have someone in mind?"

Susan replied quickly, "Who else? It's got to be a Gunderson.

There are still two left – well maybe three if you count old Abe out in Tempe, Arizona. They all at least have motive." After a moment she added, "The trouble is how in blazes did any of them do it? And for that matter what is it that they did?"

Apropos of nothing in particular JC said, "Most serial murders have a common M O. This one doesn't seem to fall in that category. If the old man was murdered – and we really don't know how he died – what did he die of? Bob was the only one to testify to the heart attack. We never even really saw the body, only the body bag that the crematorium people took off the ship. The Chicago pair were burned or asphyxiated, and these two were dashed on the rocks and/or drowned. If we should have any more we still have stabbing and shooting left as available means for the baddy, whoever he or she is."

Susan gave JC a look, "She? You think that Maude might be the guilty one?"

"I didn't say that. I just think we should never jump to conclusions," he quickly said. After a few seconds and with a glance down at the fast moving water below their vantage point he added, "I really like Maude and I would be pretty broken up if it turned out to be her."

Susan gave a sad grimace, "I'm afraid I have to agree. But like you say, all possibilities have to be on the table."

Agent O'Kelley stuck her head out the door, "Hey you two. We just got a call from the Coast Guard team that have been searching down stream for the bodies. They will be bringing them up here in a few minutes."

Ten minutes later the Coast Guard patrol craft pulled up to the dock just at their feet and several official personnel from inside the building joined the three boat crew on the dock to help with the grim cargo. Two black plastic bags containing the remains of Darrell and Clotile Darling were carefully off-loaded and carried up to the garage. Two tables had been erected by the ambulance service to receive the bodies. A medical officer was on hand to make a preliminary examination.

JC turned to Susan, "Do you want to go in and have a look?"

Susan was looking a little pale, "No. I think I'll pass. I don't think it would contribute anything to look at those two poor souls. It really gets to me. They had so much planned. They weren't very bright but they were likable and surely didn't deserve this."

They both just stood near the open door of the garage and watched the proceedings from a distance. There was a terrible fascination about the whole proceeding. They didn't really want to watch but on the other hand they couldn't tear themselves away.

After several minutes the medical team had opened the bags and had their preliminary look. O'Kelley, who had been standing close to the whole operation, broke away and came to the door.

"Just to keep you two up to date, they both died of blunt trauma effect from hitting the rocks. The medical examiner says there is no water in the lungs. They didn't drown." She screwed up her face. "I guess that's good news – if you can say there is any good news in this business. They didn't suffer much after they went over the edge."

Susan, looking very distressed said, "Yes, but how they must have suffered fighting the current and not being able to control the boat before they went over."

JC turned to the agent, "What's our move now? I imagine Captain Jack will want to get on with the trip. What else can he do?"

Agent O'Kelley thought for a minute, "I don't see any point in me joining you on the boat. I have a plate full back in Buffalo. But I would like to know if you have any suspects in mind?"

Both JC and Susan were inclined to answer. JC said, "We both are concentrating at the moment on the first mate, Bob Walden. There are a lot of reasons to believe it couldn't be him but then there are a few suspicious things that point that way. The problem is that we can't for the life of us see a motive on his part. There are plenty of reasons for suspecting a Gunderson in the business. The trouble is we are running out of Gundersons it seems."

Then more directly to them both O'Kelley asked, "Do you two really have enough experience to follow through on this business?" They both nodded assent. "Having you both on the boat should be all we need. From the inquiries I've made you seem to have made yourselves a considerable reputation. We can stay in touch by phone. Meanwhile there are a lot of details that would be better handled by me back at my office." She stood to go back into the garage; "I could come aboard at any time should you need me. The distances are not very great from here on to your final – Rhode Island, isn't it?

"What's your route from this point?"

JC said, "We traverse Lake Ontario and spend overnight at Oswego. Then the boat enters a series of canals that join up with the Erie Canal. I understand that we will be two days on the canal before we drop down into the Hudson. Then it's around Manhattan and up the East River to Rhode Island. I think we also have a stop in Manhattan for the night."

"Is that it?" asked O'Kelley.

Susan added, "We spend a night at Troy, I understand. That's right after we leave the canal."

The FBI agent retreated into the garage and the Shelbys resumed their seats on the bench beside the door. In the background they could hear the harsh rattle of static as the various components of the search teams reported in by radio. Most of it was unintelligible, muffled as it was by the walls of the building and the sound of the river at their feet. It wasn't long however before Agent O'Kelley made her reappearance.

"Just heard from one of the teams; they have recovered a major chunk of the boat. They'll be bringing it here shortly. I imagine you will want to have a look." She glanced back into the cavernous interior of the building, "Also we have something we found on the body of Mr. Darling. You may want to take a look at it."

Both JC and Susan quickly got up and entered the busy building. Susan found the atmosphere distasteful. There seemed to be more officials bustling about than were necessary. There was also an air of normality about it. She couldn't imagine anything concerning any part of this tragedy being normal. She wondered whether all these officials really cared. Of course they cared, she thought, correcting her initial response. It was just their job. They all probably did something similar to this nearly every day. That's how they earned their living. Agent O'Kelley waved them over to a counter set up along one wall. Strewed out along this surface were the contents of the clothing that the two had been wearing. It didn't amount to much. She pointed to a water soaked fragment of paper.

"Have a look at that. Be careful with it. There is not much left of it." She indicated what appeared to be about a four inch square chunk torn off a travel or advertising brochure of some kind.

JC had a look at it then asked, "Does anyone here know what it is? It looks like an advert for some business in the vicinity."

O'Kelley said, "I checked with the Coast Guard people and the police. A couple of them think it's a small restaurant and boat rental place in Sandy Beach. That's on the large island you get to just before the Falls."

Susan said, "That's where the bus stopped to let them off this morning. This pretty much confirms where they got the boat."

"It does indeed," said the agent. "But there's more. Have another look."

JC gingerly picked up the fragment and examined it closely. "I don't … Yes, I see now there are some faint pencil markings in the margin area." He peered intently at the paper, "Numbers… they look like they might be numbers."

O'Kelley remarked, "We would have been able to trace the boat easily enough but those markings may be more important. Give it a thought."

JC got a scrap of paper from his pocket and tried as carefully as he was able to copy exactly what he could see on the item. It wasn't much. The river and the Falls had done their job in an attempt to destroy all evidence. He and Susan could pore over this at leisure. Right now there was no doubt in his mind what the general course of events was: Bob Walden had given the Darlings the information about the boat rental, they had got off the bus and made their way down to the water (how, was not quite clear), rented the small motor boat, headed out into the river, and at some time later wandered into the fast moving current of the rapids that resulted in their going over the Falls. There surely must have been safeguards and warnings in place. How had these been ignored? And most importantly had those markings on the little brochure been there when Walden gave it to them or had they been scribbled by one of the Darlings at some later time? And what did those markings say?

Thirty minutes later a large Coast Guard workboat pulled up to the dock and a crew of three began the process of unloading the wreckage of the small craft that had made the big plunge. There wasn't much left. It appeared that the front half of the boat had hit the rocks first and had been more or less pulverized. The rear was not really intact but most of it had hung together and the remains of the outboard motor were still attached. The three men carried the wreckage up to the garage and carefully set it on a low platform that had been put together to aid in its examination by the experts.

JC was not an expert but he had enjoyed a brief span of his youth taking a motorboat out onto Lake Tahoe when he was a kid. His parents had vacationed there for three summers when he was in high school. He had always been allowed to rent a motorboat on these summer occasions and had had drilled into him all the necessary safety and operating knowledge needed. Maybe it was these little summer forays onto the water that had enticed him into the Navy in later life.

JC joined the group gathered around the small boat. A Coast

Guard sailor spoke up. "It's a about a 14 foot skiff. I think that motor is an Evanrude – probably a five horse"

JC had gingerly been fingering the remains of the motor. He carefully lifted it to a position that he could see under the shroud. After a few minutes of poking around he made a surprising discovery. He gestured to the Coast Guard crewman that seemed to be the expert on small boats.

"Have a look at this. This can't be right." He pointed to a spot on the plastic fuel tank.

Several of the rescue personnel present crowded around to see what was going on. The crewman stood up after a close look at what had attracted JC's attention.

"That's a hole. It looks to be about a millimeter in diameter." He had another close look. "I would be willing to bet that it's been drilled. It's a perfectly clean hole."

Another of the guardsmen present added, "I don't see how they could have gone out in that boat. The fuel would have leaked out in half an hour or so."

The skipper of the rescue boat said, "That's just what happened I'll bet."

The FBI agent gave them all a look and said, "The reason that the Shelbys and I are here is the suspicion of foul play." She had their full attention now. "I have to ask you all to regard this matter as a serious crime and to treat these physical remains as evidence." She then asked the lieutenant of the Coast Guard. "Do you have a line on the place this boat was rented? We know it was in Sandy Beach."

The lieutenant replied, "We have checked on that. I believe it had to be Halsey's Anchorage. It's a small waterside restaurant and boat rental place run by a woman named Ruth Halsey. They have only a few boats and none are very fancy. From the look of this one I would say it fits the bill as coming from her place."

Agent O'Kelley looked over at the Shelbys, "I'm betting that you two would like to come with me and see what Miss Halsey has to say. We can get her story and then I can run you on up north to your cruise ship."

On the drive back to the island and to Sandy beach O'Kelley didn't have much to say. As they pulled into the small settlement she remarked, "My bet is that it's not going to help much. A murderer, even a not very clever one, is not going to leave many clues at this place. We'll see, though."

Ruth Halsey was an elderly lady of small stature. She didn't appear to be at all happy. It was clear that she had already had some of the news at least. She knew that she had lost a boat.

Agent O'Kelley introduced herself and the two Shelbys and asked if they couldn't go inside She had a few questions. Ruth Halsey was in no position to say 'no' and curtly waved them into the tiny dining area of her establishment. The building also appeared to be her residence. As they went in JC noticed that there were no boats tied up at the small dock. There seemed to be a half dozen or so stashed in behind the building on racks. None looked like they had been in the water for some time.

Inside Halsey waved them to three chairs around a small dining table. She stood behind the fourth chair and simply gave them a hard stare.

Agent O'Kelley said, "Miss Halsey we need to ask how the boat was hired and what the circumstances were of the Darlings arrival here and their taking possession of the craft. If you could just walk us through the details, please."

Halsey didn't hesitate, "It was very simple. I got a phone call yesterday asking if I had a small motorboat that I could let a couple take out on the river. I told the man that I did. He gave me his name and said they would be here this morning. Sure enough, here they came. They paid me for a day's rental in cash and sat down at this very table and had some coffee and donuts."

"Couple of things, Miss Halsey; when the man called did he identify himself as Mr. Darling?"

"I don't recall. I just assumed that's who it was."

"Do you know where the call came from?" asked the agent.

"No. I just assumed it was from Buffalo. Where else could it be from?" she huffily replied.

O'Kelley continued, "Did you ask if they knew how to run a boat? And did you give them instructions about the hazards of the river – the rapids downstream, for example?" asked the agent.

Halsey huffed, "Of course. Everyone knows it's dangerous. You got to stay up at this end; shouldn't even go across to the other side."

O'Kelley asked, "You say 'shouldn't.' Why might they want to go to the other side?"

"Well, there's a nice beach over there, Broad Beach. A lot of folks like to picnic over there. I don't like my boats to go over there in the hands of people that don't know the river. The rapids start just below there. It's a bad place to get stranded or make a mistake."

"Do you think the Darlings might want to go over there?" asked the agent.

"I know they did. They had me fix a couple of sandwiches and two cans of pop and they said they was goin' to have a picnic. I just hope they didn't take off for that place," said Halsey.

Agent O'Kelley produced the small plastic bag containing the fragment of paper found on Darrell Darling's body and showed it to the restaurant proprietor. "Do you recognize this piece of paper?"

Halsey gingerly took the bag and held it near the window for better light. After looking at if for more than a minute she said, "Yeah, I guess I do. That's one of our little advertising leaflets. We have them out various places. Maybe he picked it up in here. I couldn't say."

O'Kelley said, "Have another look. Do you see what looks like pencil writing in the margin?"

"I don't know. It's not very clear. Looks like a bunch of numbers. Don't mean a thing to me," she answered peremptorily.

Agent O'Kelley continued, "When was the boat gassed up?

"I took 'em down to the dock with a can of gas. I filled the tank and explained how to run the motor." She hesitated, "Then they got in started her up and away they went. They seemed to know what they was doin'." The owner of Halsey's Anchorage crossed her arms over her skinny chest and demanded, "What about my boat? Do I get it back? What about damages?"

O'Kelley smiled wryly, "I assume you have insurance. There's not much left. As soon as the Coast Guard and we have finished our examination you may have a right to reclaim the remains. I can't imagine what you would do with them."

As the three bid goodbye to Ruth Halsey and started to walk to the car Susan stopped and turned to the woman who was about to reenter her establishment.

"Miss Halsey, pardon me. Would you mind pointing out Broad Beach over on the other side?" she asked.

Ruth Halsey pointed across the river. "You can just see where the beach is - that batch of trees is behind it."

Susan commented to JC, "It's a little downstream from here. I can't actually see the rapids, though."

As they walked back to the car O'Kelley filled them in on the next moves. "I will put in a call to the office when we get to the car and ask them to trace the call to this place. I don't think it will help but we have to follow every lead."

Susan asked, "Do you think it was the Mr. Darling that called?"

"I don't think we'll ever know," said the agent.

Good as her word, Siobhan O'Kelley called her office and started the process of tracking down all calls to the small restaurant. As they were driving out of the area her cell rang and she got her answers. No useful results. The call was made from a public phone near the ship in the Naval Park in Buffalo.

Susan shook her head in discouragement; "Bad luck. It could have been anybody, but my bet it was Bob Walden," then to JC, "Sweetheart, that writing on the paper. It did look like numbers.

Miss Halsey thought they might be. It was for things, figures I guess. What do you think they might be?"

The agent handed over the envelope as she drove and JC took a hard look at the scribbling in the margin. "If I had to make a guess I would say they were '8867'."

Going back to O'Kelley's latest info from her office JC added, "Why not Darrell? It could just as easily have actually been him. Why wouldn't he make the call if Bob had suggested it? What I find more intriguing at the moment is how Bob, who seems to be our prime suspect at the moment, could have got to Sandy Beach, drilled a hole, and got back to the ship. It just isn't possible. Again we have 'opportunity' missing."

Susan grinned, "Ah me! The mystery grows by the minute." Then to O'Kelley, "What do you think at this point?"

The agent laughed aloud, "I don't have any theory. I have a lot of other work to do though. You guys have all the pieces. I can't see that there is anything else but for you to rejoin the ship and for us to convince Captain Jack to carry on, steady as she goes. There is no point in disrupting the cruise any more than it has already been."

CHAPTER 12 – INTO THE ERIE

T hings never did quite get back to normal. The table that the Shelbys had shared with the Gundersons had shrunk to four; Ed and Maude, and the two amateur sleuths. The other table for reasons one could easily guess remained essentially empty. None of the other guests seem to want to redistribute themselves. Everyone seemed to huddle with their earlier accidental companions for safety. What the hazard might be no one could guess, but the mood was somber nonetheless. Even Ed and Maude seemed disinclined to converse with each other. That was not too surprising considering that they really didn't have a relationship before this cruise. Added to that must have been a completely irrational unconscious suspicion that each must have of the other.

Captain Jack put in a surprise appearance in the dining area shortly after the ship got underway in Lake Ontario. He did his best to put on a jolly face but unfortunately, unlike his first mate, Bob Walden, that was not his accustomed demeanor in the best of circumstances.

"Well folks, I hope you are all doing well this evening. Never fear, Bob is steering the ship. He is very good at it. I taught him well." He gave a slight forced chuckle. No one in the room followed suit. There was dead silence as they waited for some real news.

Captain Jack seemed to sense that something needed to be said. "Ladies and gentlemen, this has been a very sad day. I can't tell you how much I regret the discomfort and sadness you all must feel. I have given a lot of thought to what has happened and can say very little to make things better. In my view we have suffered a catastrophic series of coincidences and you have had the misfortune of having had front row seats to the whole sorry business. I don't know what we could have done that might have prevented or mitigated these disasters but why don't we all try to make the best of what time we have remaining to us on the trip.

"The best is really yet to come. This cruise was billed as a trip down the Erie Canal and that is just what we will have. Tonight we traverse the length of Lake Ontario and tomorrow we dock in the small city of Oswego, New York. It is a very pleasant town and home of one of New York's fine universities, and I highly recommend that you all get off the ship and take a little stroll around or take the bus that traverses the main street all the way through the town to the southern most outskirts. They have a wonderful supermarket there where you can do a little shopping. The bus ride makes a pleasant change from our time on the lakes. After that, in the late afternoon, we will enter the Oswego Canal that will join us up with the famous Erie, the waterway that made the northeast of this great country the engine of progress that it is. Almost immediately on entering that waterway we will traverse Lake Oneida, a very beautiful sight.

"Just a word about Lake Ontario; It is the lowest of the five lakes and with Lake Superior is of a quite different geological form from the other three. Both Ontario and Superior are quite deep; Ontario with a maximum depth of over 800 feet. In contrast Lake Erie, which we left at Buffalo, is quite shallow and contains the least water of all the five lakes. Ontario is also the gateway to the Atlantic Ocean via the Saint Lawrence Seaway. And as you all know Toronto, one of the largest cities of the North American continent with 2.6 million inhabitants, is on the north shore of the lake.

"Tomorrow we will get a run down on the Erie Canal, that fabulous engineering feat completed in 1825. Meanwhile, enjoy your meal and the evening."

With that Captain Jack gave a slight nod and retreated through the forward door. One of the male guests, the one that loved to play scrabble using his own private definitions of words, broke into song…

> *"Oh the Ery-ee is a risin*
> *And the gin is a gittin low*
> *And I scarcely think*
> *We'll git a little drink*
> *Till we git to Buffalo-oh-oh*
> *Till we git to Buffalo"*

There were a number of raised eyebrows and a few sighs but one of his pals continued –

> *"Oh the captain he came up on deck*
> *A spy glass in his hand*
> *The fog it was so tarnld thick*
> *He could scarcely see the land,*
> *Oh the Ery-ee is a risin*
> *And the gin is gittin low…"*

This did raise the spirits a little. One of the passengers suggested breaking out a bottle of gin to give the spirits just a little more corporeal form.

◊

JC and Susan retreated to the after deck after dinner to go over what they thought they had learned. It had been one of the most stressful days they had yet experienced – well, barring the sinking of the MS Nevsky off New Zealand, but who is counting? They both had become quite inured to a certain level of disaster occurring in their daily lives. Some people just seem to attract excitement. These little reviews that they conducted from time to time constituted the real secret of their detecting success.

They found a secluded corner that afforded quiet and security and gave them a fabulous view of the sunset sky to the west.

Susan began, "We really fell into it this time. Do you suppose we are a magnet for trouble in some mysterious way? I can't believe that everywhere we go these things seem to happen."

JC smiled and said, "No, I don't believe we are any kind of cause, but you know how statistics works. Take the sad examples that we see all the time in news stories where a perfectly decent family will lose two or three of their children in totally unrelated accidents through absolutely no fault of their own. It's a rare occurrence but we read about it often because it is shocking and seems so irrational. We always say, 'How could that happen to such nice people?'

"If you believed in destiny you would attribute it to some mysterious force working in our favor to promote our careers."

Susan screwed up her face, "That is a particularly ghoulish thing to say."

"Hey, Susan dear, you are the one that is always on the lookout for the next corpse," he rejoined.

She pouted, "You make me sound just awful."

"You aren't awful. You're darned marvelous. Let's drop that. Now what about the Gunderson mystery? Got any ideas?"

Susan joked, "My main idea at the moment is that I am really glad I am not a Gunderson." Then more seriously, "I can't get it out of my mind that Bob Walden has to be the one. The only other candidates are Ed and Maude. Neither one of them has had any more opportunity than Walden though. Can you think of anyone else?"

"I went over the passenger list pretty carefully," said JC. "I had O'Kelley speak with the captain. He is now well aware of our position on board. From all I could find out. There isn't a single person on board other than the Gundersons themselves who would profit from these deaths."

Susan said fearfully, "It is kind of spooky. What if profit is not the motive? What if it's some kind of insane thing – a fixation or something? Maybe somebody on board is allergic to the name Gunderson, or hates people that gather in bunches of seven."

JC couldn't resist laughing at that, "Pardon me dear, that's the dumbest thing I ever heard."

"Please don't call me dumb until you come up with a better idea," said Susan. Then getting back on track, "Now we still have Walden as prime. He clearly was the one that sent the Chicago Gundersons off to the play and the Darlings off to the boat rental. That has to be pretty damning."

"It may be damning but it won't hold up in court," said JC. "I think we are at a dead end for the moment. Let's give it a rest. Maybe something will turn up."

"I hope it's not another body," said Susan. She was quiet for at least five minutes then said, "We do have a clue – the number 8867. That's got to have a meaning. It really doesn't matter who wrote it on the restaurant ad. It wasn't put there by the printer and the Darlings seemed to need or want it."

JC didn't reply. He had no answer.

Susan said, "I'm going to sleep on it and dream of 8867's all night. Maybe something will turn up. Maybe it's a prime number."

JC really laughed this time, "What would you know about prime numbers?"

Susan gave him a punch on the arm, "As much as you. I don't think I have ever heard you even mention them."

In mock seriousness JC said, "I haven't had a great deal of use for them lately."

Susan smirked quietly, "I actually think it is a prime number."

◊

There wasn't much going on aboard and most of the passengers had an early night. The ship was docked the next morning alongside the pier at the northern end of the main street of Oswego, New York. The passengers scattered off the ship for a stroll around the town. The actual business section of the town was quite a walk but there were regular busses that traversed the city and most used them. Moored near the *Chicago Belle* was an old army patrol boat that was maintained as a museum ship. The Shelbys decided to take the bus to the end of the line. This gave them a view of the city and a chance to have a look at the canal on which they would soon to be making their way alongside the highway. When they left the bus the driver cautioned them to be at the stop on the hour. That was the schedule – one bus per hour – and if they didn't want to miss the sailing they had better be there.

Susan told her husband that she wanted to buy a fly-swatter at the grocery store. JC laughed heartily.

"A fly-swatter! What in the world would you want a fly-swatter for?"

"To swat flies and mosquitoes," she answered. "Haven't you noticed? When we came in to the dock today there seemed to be a distinct increase in insect life in the vicinity of the ship. The weather is warm and we like to keep our cabin door open. Besides we are about to do two days in a very narrow canal probably with nothing but farms and woods alongside. It's just a precaution," she smiled sweetly and gave him a peck on the cheek.

JC decided that Susan could do as she liked, provided it could be easily transported. He would put his foot down if she were to suddenly be attracted to a set of dishes or cookware. He had no intention of carrying that back.

◊

The ship got underway into the Oswego Canal at 3:30 as scheduled. This broad waterway was filled with local activity. People gathered on the outside decks to see the passing sights and to begin to soak up the ambiance of the purpose of the cruise – a voyage down a very famous canal, really a complex system of canals. Bob did not make an appearance, but his voice did come booming out of the outside deck speakers with the information they needed to follow their progress. He explained that the Oswego Canal was actually a very short waterway that joined up after a few miles with the famed Erie just before they entered Lake Oneida. Bob also pointed out that the original Erie Canal began construction at Rome, New York and took advantage of a number of existing waterways, including the Mohawk River. If one wanted to follow the full journey of the 19th century barges you would begin your journey in Buffalo. Teams of horses or mules towed the barges. This explained why that long initial leg of the journey was not in Lake Ontario itself but was confined to the canals. The *Chicago Belle* would actually only be doing half the Erie. His short speech ended with the not too happy news that the sun deck above the main cabin and lounge was to be secured until they entered the Hudson River at the end of the canal. The first mate explained that the ship had been specially constructed to enable it to pass under the very large number of bridges that carried roadways over the Erie. This necessitated taking down the protective railings, and folding and storing all the umbrellas, chairs and tables.

CHAPTER 13 –
AN ERIE DEATH

The first day on the canal was devoted to hanging over the rails fore and aft to take in the close at hand sights of northern New York State. It is a green and pleasant landscape and was home to a great deal of the early history of the United States. Bob came on the speaker often to call attention to various landmarks. The travelers aboard the small vessel heard stories about Saratoga, Oriskany, Iroquois, and a bewildering number of Indian place names and tribes – some that fought with the British and others with the American Revolutionaries.

During one of their breaks in the sightseeing activities JC and Susan took time out to relax in the largely deserted lounge. Susan had been only half attentive to what was passing by on the banks of the waterway. She had been doing some of her accustomed intuitive sleuthing. They had found a small couch in a back corner that was definitely out of the way and nearly private.

"JC, I've been thinking." JC gave a grin. This was standard Susan procedure for the beginning of one of their analytical dialogues. "That piece of paper, the bit from the restaurant flyer."

"Did you dream about 8867?" he jokingly responded.

"No, but I think I have an idea." She sat up on the couch and asked, "Do you suppose the captain has some maps of the water-ways around here? He must have. You couldn't run a boat without a good map collection."

JC grinned, "I think they are called charts, sweetie, and I'm sure he has a complete set up front in the wheel house, or bridge or whatever they call it."

"Some sailor you are. You'll have to help me. Let's go up there and have a look." Then she hastened to add, "Let's not tell Bob. He is still a main suspect and I would just as soon he not get in on our ideas just yet."

They got off the couch and made their way up to the bow of the ship. The door opening into the small bridge from the outside deck was shut but they could see that it was Captain Jack manning the wheel at the moment. Bob Walden was not in evidence. The Captain welcomed them into the cramped space and inquired as to their mission. He was well aware by now that they represented the law as far as the accumulation of crimes and tragedies that had occurred.

He responded to their query, "There is a small space just behind here where all the navigation is done. There is a chart table in there and you will find all the charts in the large drawers under the table. Help yourself." He concentrated for a moment on his steering in passing a small boat headed the other way then, "what particular area are you interested in?"

"The river above the Falls - specially the area across from Sandy beach and on into the rapids area," said Susan.

The captain told them which drawer would have those charts and told them to take their time. He then turned back to guiding the vessel.

Susan and JC managed to find just the chart she said she needed and spread it out on the large flat navigation table. JC pointed out the exact location of Halsey's Anchorage.

Susan then said, pointing to the spot and indicating a line from that point across the river, "right over there should be Broad Beach."

JC peered at the map, "I don't see it marked. It really doesn't show much about landmarks. It looks like it is mainly about the water and the shore contour." He pointed a little to the north and noted, "There are the rapids. That is what they were supposed to stay away from."

"Okay," said Susan, "I figure that what was written on that flyer was not 8867 but BB 67. BB could just be shorthand for Broad Beach. They said they wanted to picnic there."

JC smiled, "I get it. 67 is a compass heading from the restaurant dock."

JC thought for a minute. "Wait a minute let's see that map again." He gave it a quick look and said, "The river runs dead west at the location of Broad Beach. That means that notation had to mean relative heading to the direction of the river's current from Halsey's place. We can forget about a compass. I think a bit of hand waving would have done. I don't see why anyone would pick a number like 67. I guess we will never know at this point."

They put the chart away and exited through the wheelhouse thanking Captain Jack on the way. He asked if they had found what they needed. Affirmative, they assured him. They found a spot at the side rail where they could talk near their cabin.

Susan began, "Here is the way I see it. Bob made the reservation by phone and let it seem that he was Darrell Darling. It doesn't matter whether he or Darrell actually made the call. The result is the same. Then Bob gave the leaflet to Darrell and either told him how to get to Broad Beach or actually jotted the numbers in the margin himself. Since you can't actually see Broad Beach from the dock there at Halsey's he would have to have told them a compass bearing."

JC, said, "I can't argue with a word of that. I think you are dead on. I noted that the map is pretty clear about the rapids and even has barriers and warnings noted. Getting to Broad Beach would be cutting it pretty close."

Susan frowned in thought for several minutes, "You know, JC, if that tank of gas held out to get them over there and they had their picnic then I guess there would still be a danger when they got ready to start back. By that time it surely would have been pretty well gone. What if it had truly run out? They would be stranded. That clearly didn't happen but what if it had?"

JC had an answer for that, "I believe our murderer must have a whole series of alternative plans ready for any contingency. Why not? He or she has the whole cruise to find other opportunities for doing any of them in. For forty million dollars you can afford to make a few extra detailed plans."

Susan then added, "Oh, by the way, when you speak with O'Kelley ask her to have the medical examiner do an autopsy. It might be useful to know whether they had that picnic or not."

◊

The two of them had soon talked out all the details they could think of and decided it was time for a little sleep. The ship had come to a stop alongside a quiet piece of countryside and had tied up for the night. The cruise would not cover any appreciable distances in the dark. First it wasn't exactly safe since obstructions and problems couldn't be easily avoided, and second the cruise company didn't want any of their clients to miss the beauty of Upstate New York. This part of the country is well settled and very picturesque and largely unappreciated by most citizens. It is also the site of a great deal of the early history of the country. From the War for Independence through the opening of the Erie Canal in 1826 it was probably most critical piece of real estate on the continent.

JC had no trouble falling dead asleep. The same was not true for Susan. She couldn't get it out of her mind that she might be missing something. To date everything seemed so pat. It was hard to avoid suspecting Bob Walden, and yet he must know that. Some kind of double game must be underway. She just couldn't figure out what it was. How could he expect to literally get away with murder? So far it looked like all it required was an ironclad excuse concerning opportunity. Motive was obviously weak too – that is, unless someone was paying him. That possibility would have to include one of the Gundersons. If he were aiding a Gunderson the rewards could be very rich indeed. The trouble was they were running short on Gundersons. Surely it couldn't be dear Maude or quiet little Ed. Yes – of course, it could be either one. Then there was even one more Gunderson; the one in Tempe, Arizona. Why hadn't anyone had much to say about him? He seemed like a ghostly figure sort of floating uninterested and uninteresting in the background.

These ruminations were buzzing annoyingly around in Susan's head when a competing distraction began to intrude. She could just make out a voice – a single voice – not a conversation. It sounded a little like somebody having a heated conversation with themselves. It wasn't loud though. Everyone had taken to their beds and the ship was very quiet. The piece of canal that they sat in was flat and silent as a lake. No noises intruded from the shore and yet there was this buzz of conversation – one-sided conversation.

She finally decided it must be coming from the dining lounge. Their cabin opened onto the outside deck passageway just a few feet from the entrance to the lounge. Voices nearly always carried easily the short distance and could be heard if their door was left open.

Susan being Susan decided she should investigate. There was no sense in disturbing JC. He needed his sleep – or so she thought. Actually, though, she liked to venture into these little secret places in their investigations on her own. Sometimes the results turned out rather badly. She had had two hospital visits on account of this peculiarity of hers; one in Hawaii and one in Colorado. She couldn't legitimately count the time when she was drugged in London and spirited off to Saint Petersburg, Russia. She wasn't actually injured in that caper even though she managed to get herself separated from JC by a few thousand miles and a great many days.

What harm could a mysterious voice in a darkened dining lounge in the middle of the night do? Why none at all is the way her reasoning went. So she decided to see what was up. In her bare feet and wearing just pajamas she crept the few steps to the door into the dining area. There were some very dim lights inside over the doors to assist anyone needing to find their way in the dark. She decided these would be sufficient for her to make out whatever action might be taking place in there.

She quietly stepped inside and stood with her back to the closed door and concentrated on trying to make out who might be present other than herself. It wasn't long before her eyes were adapted to the low level of light that prevailed and she could make out a figure at the forward end of the room. The figure was standing facing the wall and seemed to be gesticulating wildly. The person was apparently a man. She could hear the fear in his voice apparently talking to no one in particular. Straining as intently as possible she could simply not make out anyone else in the room, and at first she had no idea who the man might be. She stood stock-still and listened. It slowly dawned on her that she did indeed know who it was; it was Ed Gunderson. This was no great surprise. If something odd was going to happen it had to happen to or around someone in the Gunderson clan.

Susan was very confused at this point. She didn't know whether she should make her presence known or to simply be quiet and see if the situation might resolve itself. In the end she decided she should wait and try to find out what was actually going on.

Ed was very perturbed and was obviously carrying on a conversation with an unseen adversary. The trouble was there was no one else in the room except Susan who stood at least thirty feet behind him at the door to the deck. The wall in front of him held no clue. Or did it? The more Susan stared at the scene the more details emerged. There was something on the wall in front of Ed – a large mirror. Susan had noticed it when they first came aboard. It was right next to the door to the forward passageway on the right. It was installed just behind and above a counter that usually held the various brochures that they could pick up describing points of interest and usually also held a large decorative bouquet of flowers.

Ed was obviously in something of a deranged state and seemed to be talking to his own reflection. From time to time he would wildly wave his arms or shake his fist at the mirror. Finally Susan decided an intervention was in order.

"Mr. Gunderson - Ed!" she spoke out fairly loudly. "Can I help you?"

Ed Gunderson jumped back and whirled around screaming, "Get away! Get away! He'll kill you."

His insane behavior really frightened Susan and in spite of herself she shied away. Ed came at her bare-footed in his pajamas shouting and waving at her. She really thought she might get hurt so she backed out the door onto the deck. It wasn't a moment and she found herself, not at the door of her cabin, but at the aft rail of the rear observation deck. Ed rounded the back corner of the cabin and came charging at her. She was genuinely frightened by this time. No one seemed about to appear on the scene to rescue her. Actually only seconds had passed since he had begun his outburst.

Susan was not up to wrestling with a fit farmer regardless of the fact that he was in his seventies and threw up her arms to defend herself. Ed grabbed at her and she frantically kept backing away. He was screaming and shouting all the time. He made one final mighty lunge at her and came up hard against the aft rail as she ducked under his arm. The momentum of his charge toppled him over the edge of the rail. Susan could see he was about to go into the canal behind the ship and made a desperate effort to grab him and keep him on board. It didn't work. She got a hold of the leg of his pajama, which ripped off in her hand, as he plunged over the side.

She began yelling at the top of her voice, "Man overboard! Man overboard!" She didn't know what else to do.

Lights began to come on up and down the ship and it wasn't even half a minute before two of the student crew were on hand. Captain Jack showed up five seconds later and took charge. A life ring was dragged out of a bench and thrown over the side. The captain and the two crew headed for the gangway with arms loaded with lines and some inflatable devices to see if they could get poor Ed out of the water before he drowned. It was fast work on their part. In less than five minutes they had the still form of Ed laid out on the grassy slope beside the ship. By this time Bob Walden had come on the scene and had turned on all the ship's outside lights to assist in the rescue. Passengers had come out of their cabins, most in their nightwear, and were lining the rail to watch the proceedings. So far Ed had not responded to any of the emergency treatment that was being provided.

Thirty minutes later all could hear the siren of the approaching emergency vehicle sent out on the call from the nearby city of Rome, New York. The uniformed personnel bustled about and gathered up the still motionless figure and got him into the ambulance. The Captain and his assistants gathered up their paraphernalia and boarded. Susan and JC could see the grim look on Captain Jack's face and he was shaking his head. He also was not talking to anyone. Several of the passengers tried to query him but he shrugged them off with a stern look that discouraged the ones behind them.

A lot of the people drifted back into their cabins but a dozen, at least, gathered in the lounge to gossip about the strange event. Susan and JC stayed behind alone on the rear deck and decided to talk a bit there and look over the scene. Maybe they would come up with a clue or even just an idea.

"What happened, Susan?"

"I couldn't sleep and I kept hearing this voice. It sounded like a one-sided conversation. I decided it was coming from the lounge so I quietly went out on the deck, stepped back there, and looked in. It was Ed at the front of the lounge talking to the wall I thought at first. Ed saw something. I think he was looking in the mirror and was arguing with his own reflection. It sounds weird, doesn't it?" she said.

"Then what," asked JC?

"Well – I spoke up and he sort of went nuts and attacked me," she answered.

JC didn't say anything for quite a while.

Susan with serious worry in her voice said, "JC, I didn't push him over the side."

JC gave a slight amused snort, "Susan, sweetheart, I never thought for an instant that you did. It's just strange that a person could fall into the water, be pulled out in a matter of minutes, and apparently not appear to recover somewhat." With a change of tone, "You did notice when they took him away he looked pretty out of it. Somehow it doesn't seem reasonable. I would put money on the fact that he was probably dead when he went over the rail, or nearly so, and that the fall into the water had nothing to do with it." He gave her a bright look. "What do you think?"

Susan gave a weak smile, "I love you JC. Even if I were a murderer, I know I could always depend on you. No, of course I didn't push him and it is obvious to me that he was pretty high or whatever you call it. He was seeing things – things that were not too pleasant." She thoughtfully continued, "I wonder. I wonder what would be really unpleasant for Ed?"

◊

The next morning JC gave a call on his cell phone to their FBI partner in Buffalo. Siobhan O'Kelley thanked them for the information and informed them that she would be on to the authorities in Rome with the information they would need for instigating a thorough medical evaluation of the situation. She mentioned also that the small boat did have a cheap compass. She also told them that she would call

Captain Jack and advise him to continue his trip on schedule. There was no point in sitting still in the canal in the middle of New York for no particular purpose. They were soon underway, breakfast was served, and aside from a lot of subdued but horrified buzz in the dining salon, nothing much was going on. The Shelbys decided to hang out on the forward deck. They couldn't think of anything better to do. Maybe an idea would occur to one of them. If they stayed together and an idea did come flying out the other one would be there to catch it.

It wasn't long before they had company. Maude made an appearance. She looked terrible. Her face was streaked and it appeared that she had even forgotten to comb her hair after rising. JC motioned her over and offered her a chair. Wordlessly she plopped herself into it and immediately put her head down into her hands.

Susan pulled her chair up close and put her arm over the woman's shoulder. "Maude, dear, it has been just awful. Please stay close by we will try to look after you." Susan looked up, appealing to JC. He didn't know quite what to do. Comforting ladies in situations like this was just a little out of his area of expertise. JC did put a hand over her hands, which she had dropped to her lap.

Finally Maude managed a few words. "I don't know what to do. I'm scared – scared to death."

The Shelbys were scared too. Neither one of them could come up with much in the way of consolation. Just being with her seemed the right thing at the moment.

Finally Susan said, "Look, Maude, we are going to try and look after you. Until this trip is over we'll all just stay together." She thought for a minute and then added, "I don't believe that JC and I are in any danger. So far it has been a Gunderson thing." She gave Maude a little squeeze; "I don't blame you for worrying. Who wouldn't?"

Maude sat up and forcefully announced, "I'm leaving this death trap in New York. I'll be home then and I think I'll be all right. I don't care what the damned will says. As far as I can see all bets are off – or they should be. I don't even know who the lawyer is that we were all supposed to see." She was quiet for a minute, then, "He can just come and see me in New York if he wants to. I don't need anything; just a chance to be home and safe." She started to weep, "God, this is awful – all dead. I can't believe it."

JC said, "Maude, we're just outside Rome. You could fly home if you wanted to. You could be home before the day is out."

"No," replied Maude, "I actually would feel better staying on with you two. I don't think I could stand the airport hassle and trying to get from Kennedy or LaGuardia to my apartment by myself. The ship docks at 55th and that is only steps away from my flat." Then, after a moment, "You don't mind, do you?"

Susan cried, "of course not. I think I would feel the same. Maybe we can get the captain or somebody to change your cabin to the one next to ours. I'm sure that couple wouldn't mind moving. It's not like the ship is chock full." Only after she said this did the macabre nature of her remark strike home. She blushed.

◊

The ship got under way with an announcement by Bob over the speaker system. His jolly tone and the spewing out of irrelevant information about the countryside they were passing through seemed incongruous in the extreme considering the circumstances. No one seemed to be listening and most were huddled in the lounge trying to look nonchalant, poring through magazines mindlessly, probably with dark thoughts streaming through their heads. The Shelbys and Maude were still on the forward deck when Captain Jack stepped out of the wheelhouse and approached.

"Shelby's and Mrs. Snyder, I saw you out here and thought you might like a report from the Rome police."

"We certainly would," replied Susan. What have they found out? Do they know what killed poor Ed?"

"They do indeed," he answered. "It was poison. A very unusual kind of poison – also very famous, I believe."

JC frowned, "Oh, how so?"

"They found pseudaconitine, known also as nepaline," he said.

Susan said, "That doesn't tell us much."

Maude interjected, "It comes from monk's hood, a plant famous for doing away with folks, especially in India."

The captain continued, "It seems the behavior you witnessed, Mrs. Shelby, would not be unusual for someone who had ingested a fatal dose."

Maude paled, "Someone on this ship put the stuff in his food. We're all in danger."

JC said with some ill-considered irony, "Apparently only you, Maude."

Susan was furious, "Shut up JC. What are you trying to do to the poor woman?"

The captain then turned to Maude, "Mrs. Snyder, I have asked Richard, our cook, to specially prepare all your food and make sure no one touches it until he serves it to you." He continued somewhat ruefully, "There are other hazards, however, as we've seen." He gave her a hard look. "Would you like to leave the ship at this point and fly home?"

"No, I'm going to stay with my friends here and under your protection. Somehow I think I will be better off."

Captain Jack bowed slightly and reentered the wheelhouse. Through the glass of its windows they could see that Bob was at the wheel and seemed to be concentrating diligently on steering the ship. How odd it all seemed. Who might the depraved murderer be - Bob, Maude who?

After they were alone again Maude volunteered some information that neither of the Shelbys had been aware of – the history of nepaline poison, also known as aconitine.

"During the Indian rebellion of 1857," she explained, "Some

native chefs tried to poison the British officers, but were found out. The food was given to a monkey who died on the spot, and the British forced the cooks to take the poison. This managed to do them all in. Both Oscar Wilde and James Joyce made use of the stuff in their writings – a powerful and famous potion."

CHAPTER 14 –
INTO THE HUDSON

Fortunately for the whole ships company the remainder of their trip along the canal was relatively uneventful. The passengers were gradually getting back their good spirits and were taking an interest in the passing scenery. Of particular interest were the final series of locks that were to drop them down into the magnificent Hudson River. Bob explained to them through a series of short lectures over the speaker system that the builders of the canal had been stalled at the top of the hill that looked down to the Hudson for some time by the financial interests of the wagon companies that made their living by carrying the goods from the end of the canal down to the barges on the river. This impasse was soon overcome and a series of locks completed by 1826 that dropped the canal down to the Hudson at Troy, New York. Using the Mohawk River, a major tributary of the Hudson, for a better part of the last third of t he canal was an enormous advantage

At the top of the hills that lined the river one could look out over the bow of the ship and see the descent to the broad waters of the Hudson. It was a breathtaking sight. Another of the sights that occurred from time to time were occasional glimpses of the old original canal through the trees and brush that lined the newer and much broader modern waterway. No modern barge or ship could possibly fit into those original narrow passages or the small locks.

After dinner on the second day spirits were eventually raised sufficiently that the dining lounge singer was back in business -

"......

Oh, the cook she was a grand old gal,
She wore a spotted dress,
They hoisted her upon the mast,
As a signal of distress,
Oh, the Ery-ee was a risin,
And the gin was a gittin low,
…..."

◊

The announcement came near the end of the next day that the ship would be tied up beside the riverfront park in Troy for the evening and then would be anchored out in the river for the night. Bob explained that the trip down the Hudson and the approach to Manhattan was probably the most scenic voyage on the North American continent. The ship would take advantage of the full day for the scenic sightseeing and a brief stop at West Point, the Army's officer training academy that was hard on the east bank of the river just above New York City. Early American painters couldn't get enough of depicting scenes of the broad Hudson and its gently rising wooded mountains that lined both banks.

The evening in Troy was entertaining. Everyone went ashore and joined the city residents in the park for music, eats and all sorts of fun. There was a band, dancing and several entertainers. Food vendors were set up all over the area and the whole was only steps away from the gangway off the ship. Late that night with everyone aboard, the ship put out into the middle of the river and anchored.

Bob explained that this was just a precaution. Vandals had been known to try and board vessels tied up in the city center in the past.

Troy itself was an important part of the country's history. It was once a rival of Pittsburg as the producer of the country's steel. In its heyday, during the early years of the 20th century, its population topped 70,000. Today the city had a bare 50,000 inhabitants and various schemes to revitalize the local economy had had dubious results. The shining jewel of Troy today is the Rensselaer Polytechnic Institute.

◊

On the following day nearly all the passengers of the *Chicago Belle* were present on the upper sun deck. The crew had reinstalled the rails and had set up the tables, chairs, chaise lounges and umbrellas – no more low bridges. The three-student crew was busy making multiple trips to the kitchen for snacks and drinks for most of the day.

Aside from the brief visit to West Point there was very little evidence of civilization along the river. It seemed odd being this close to the largest city of the continent. There did appear briefly a low flying Piper Cub, probably from the nearby Reinbeck historical museum airfield. It didn't make a great deal of noise and was moving at a leisurely pace. It seemed to fit the gentle mood of the river on this warm summer afternoon.

JC and Susan had commandeered a pair of lounge chairs and a shaded table. Susan had decided to take a nap and was fast asleep in her chair. JC was fascinated by the passing unspoiled native landscape and was just sitting quietly gazing off to the shore. They had a visitor.

Maude approached and asked, "Mind if I sit with you for a little?"

"Of course not, please do," replied JC.

Susan opened an eye and smiled, "Hi, Maude, please join us. As you can see we are not very busy," she laughed.

JC waved to Up Chuck who just happened to be passing. "Hey Up, how about some iced tea and whatever you have down there for eats – not much mind you." He turned to Maude, "Maude, what would you like?"

The student grinned and stood by waiting for orders. They finally settled on a few sandwiches and the aforementioned iced tea.

Maude opened the conversation, "Shelbys, you've both been very good to me." She hesitated briefly, "I suspect that you have been in touch with the authorities and are working on this awful situation." Her face betrayed her distress. "I just have to tell you that I don't envy you task and I'm really very sorry for you – and for everyone's misfortune in having gotten mixed up with the Gundersons."

JC thought it might be wise to clue Maude into the role of the Shelby's. "Maude, we haven't broadcast it but it probably has been obvious that we have spent a deal of time with police and the like. Actually we are helping out the FBI. An agent from Buffalo, Siobhan O'Kelley, has us on the look out here aboard the *Chicago Belle*. We worked with her all day there at the Falls."

Susan had a merry look in her eye. "Maude, you `know it's really our fault. JC and I seem to attract trouble. It's happened before – many times. Some day when the history of our exploits is written, scholars will ponder over the question – why did the Shelbys manage to attract so much trouble and crime?"

Maude gave a small chuckle, "Well, I know that's not true." Taking a new tack, "But that is not what I have to tell you today." She nibbled at her sandwich, "I really am leaving the ship in Manhattan just as I said earlier. I don't see any point in riding up the coast to Rhode Island. I've had enough." She was quiet and thoughtful for several long seconds. "You know I really didn't know any of these people. I may be related but I never knew them. Of course, I am dreadfully sorry for what has happened but no more sorry than I would be if they were just random strangers – which they were indeed."

JC asked, "What about the inheritance or whatever it is?"

Maude said, "I have plenty of money and a nice place to live. I have a few friends – people I've known for years - mostly colleagues of my husband's. I really don't need or want any part of the Gunderson money. When we dock in Manhattan I will be saying goodbye." She put her hand on Susan's and continued, "You two have made it possible for me to stay sane for these past few days and I really thank you for being my friends."

JC said, "I think we stay the night docked in Manhattan. I will see you to your apartment."

Maude laughed, "Thanks, JC, but I'm an old hand around there. I'll just take a cab when we dock this evening." She stood and excused herself. "I'm going to go to my cabin and get things packed up. I'll see you at supper."

CHAPTER 15 – MANHATTAN

The ship put in at one of the several docks that constituted New York's cruise facilities. The Hudson River was nothing like it was in the old days with its industry and cargo docks almost the full length of the island. Today it was parks, recreation facilities, and museums along nearly the whole shore. The newly developed cruise line facilities, able to service several ships at a time, made the Hudson River embankment a recreational goal for New Yorkers and tourists alike.

It was nearly dark when the ship docked. Maude had her suitcase near the gangway and was prepared to debark and make her way to her apartment that overlooked Central Park - a very elegant neighborhood. JC and Susan were with her.

JC insisted in seeing her shore and safely on her way home. She protested it was no trouble at all. She would just get a cab and be home in minutes. The location of the dock at 49th Street and 12th Avenue was almost next door to the park. It happened to be raining. Clouds had come up late in the day and a gently rain had begun about an hour before they arrived. It was now coming down fairly hard. Maude said she wouldn't get wet but JC insisted even more strongly that he would see her into a cab. He carried her case out to the street and was prepared to tuck her safely into her transportation. There were no cabs present however. It was a bad hour of the evening and no other ships were docked. The *Chicago Belle* was a small ship carrying few passengers, none of whom would normally be debarking here, so cabs were all busy elsewhere apparently.

Maude could see it was futile to stand here getting wet so she gestured across the way and said, "JC just get my case over there to the bus stop. I know the buses and they run very frequently. There is some shelter there and I will be just as well off on the bus as in a cab." He started to protest but she said vigorously, "Let's go," and started off leaving him at the curb. He hurried after her and they managed to get in out of the rain in the rudimentary bus shelter.

The bus appeared minutes later and the last JC saw of her she was just getting seated and was attempting to wave to him through the rain streaked window next to her seat.

When he got back aboard, somewhat bedraggled by his foray into the rain he was met inside at the gangway entrance by Susan.

"JC, I got a phone call on the ship's line while you were out. Siobhan, our FBI friend, is in town and wants to see us before we sail in the morning. I told her to come any time. She said she would come this evening and will be here in about a half hour."

JC said, "Do you know what she wants? She's a long way from home."

Susan gave a smile, "Well not really. Buffalo *is* in New York I believe. She didn't say; maybe just to review what we know to date."

As they went up the stairs to the lounge JC said, "We'll grab a bite and just hang out here." Then he asked, "Did you tell Captain Jack?"

"I'm pretty sure he knows. He took the call and called me to the phone. I'm sure they had a few words before I got there," she said.

It seemed only minutes before the petite little Irish FBI agent appeared through the front door of the lounge. She was not dressed in her on duty 'investigating' outfit. This evening it was slacks, a waterproof parka, and a slouchy looking rain hat. JC didn't doubt there was a gun somewhere under that stuff, as unlikely as it might appear. She gave them a cheery greeting and the three of them sat in a small relatively private nook at the back. Other passengers were huddled on couches and chairs watching the TV. Tonight was Thursday and comedies were on, beginning with *The Big Bang Theory*.

They told O'Kelley that Maude had left the ship and was probably home by now. She looked just little worried.

"I would have preferred that she waited. We could have delivered her safely to her door," she commented.

JC said that he thought it was okay. She seemed to know the bus system like the back of her hand.

Susan changed the subject, "I don't think we know any more than we knew back at Rome. Have you learned anything new?"

O'Kelley said, "Not really. Tests proved that it was aconitine that killed Ed Avery. We have no idea how he managed to ingest it. The police took samples everywhere they could think of. There wasn't a trace of it on the ship. We even had a look at the first aid supplies down in the first mate's quarters."

Susan's face lit up briefly, "By the way, Siobhan, I have something I need to give you. I don't know if it's important – I doubt it actually – but you ought to have everything. Wait here a second. It's in the cabin."

She left and returned with a small plastic bag, which she proceeded to hand over. "There's a note inside describing where and when I picked this up. Like I said, it's probably not relevant. I got it off the table at dinner the night that Avery died."

O'Kelley smiled, "Susan, you would be surprised what is and is not important. Hardly anything falls in the 'is not' category. Thanks. I'll hang on to it."

The agent stood to go. JC said, "The ship sails early in the morning. We are supposed to be docking in Rhode Island about midday."

◊

It was after breakfast the next day just as they were passing the UN building on the East Shore of Manhattan that JC's cell phone rang. The two of them were out on the sun deck at the time. The rain had quit and the day looked like it might turn out clear and warm. After listening to the caller a few minutes he put the phone away and turned to Susan with an agonized look on his face.

"Susan, that was O'Kelley. Maude has disappeared. She never arrived at her apartment."

CHAPTER 16 –
THE END?

The shock was profound, especially for poor JC. He had let her go on the bus. It was a very short ride. What could possibly have happened? They should have been forewarned. Every one of these awful killings had been difficult to understand. None of them had a logical explanation as to opportunity. He immediately headed forward along the passageway to the bridge. He had to let Captain Jack know. As he approached the side window of the bridge he slowed, making sure that it was the captain in the wheelhouse and not Bob. The first mate had not been in evidence since his morning spiel as they had rounded the south end of Manhattan.

Captain Jack motioned him into the bridge when he caught sight of him. JC gave him the news as briefly as possible.

"What should we do, Captain?" JC said in a low tortured voice.

Jack Waite had a grim look as JC spoke, "JC, What can we do? I have to get this ship home and there is nothing for it but to keep going. It's not far. It's about a 160 miles. We'll be there by midafternoon if I can keep this tub above twenty knots. I suggest we keep mum about this latest. It is not going to do any of the passengers any good to know." He shrugged and gripped the wheel more tightly as he stared out ahead. "The company has already taken a big hit by this awful business."

JC stood in agonized silence for a long minute, "You know, Captain, I should have been able to stop this carnage. Susan and I were pretty cocky when we first thought we had a crime on board." He looked hard at nothing on the deck at his feet. "In Cleveland we knew we had a serious problem. I can't help but believe we could have done something at that point." He gave the captain a stare, "You know we have a mad man on board. None of us are safe."

The captain said, "There is not much I can do but we might take some precautions. Do you and your wife have any real suspicions?"

"Yes," said JC. "For some time now we have thought Bob Walden may have had a hand, but I'm sure you might have guessed the problem."

The captain frowned questioningly.

"Opportunity!" said JC. "Bob always seemed to be happily somewhere else when bad things happened, except of course at the Falls." After a hesitation, "But even there, somebody had to go ashore to Halsey's and prepare that boat for its demise."

Captain Jack had one last comment; "If it's all right I'm going to let Fenwick Bender, old Fender Bender, keep an eye on Bob for the rest of the day. He has quite a reputation at Brown. I understand he plays right guard on the varsity and he's plenty smart as well – straight A. I shouldn't actually use that term I hear. Someone told me it's pass or fail at Brown."

JC said, "It's late in the game. Even so, I can't see anything but good in that. Go ahead and put him on it." Then ruefully, "There's no one left to kill."

The captain gave a macabre laugh, "No one but the Shelbys."

◊

The afternoon did pass pleasantly. Most of the passengers spent their time getting their bags packed and in between time sunning themselves on the upper sun deck. Lucy and Up were kept very busy driving the company further and further into the red with their servings of drinks and eats in a steady stream throughout the day.

It was a matter of universal interest that brought everyone out on deck when they entered Narragansett Bay. The water was dotted with activity and the *Chicago Belle* had to follow a carefully charted path through a maze of fishing craft and lobster pot markers floating nearly everywhere and avoiding the underwater hazard of a recently sunken freighter of unknown and mysterious identity. Bob came on the speakers again to enthusiastically announce the details of their arrival. He pointed out that this bay is not really a bay but the largest estuary in the country with millions of gallons of freshwater pouring in daily from the Sakonnet and Taunton Rivers. It was certainly a complex seaway with over thirty islands scattered about.

The ship finally docked at a small pier that looked to be located in a semi-rural area. There were no signs of a sizeable city in evidence. Everyone knew, of course, that Providence was nearby and their planes and homebound transport were within easy reach by taxi or bus. A woman who appeared to be one of the cruise lines senior officials greeted the passengers on the small dock. She gave each person as they came down the gangplank a handshake and warm greeting to Rhode Island and offered personal assistance in their onward journeys. JC and Susan waited until everyone has left the ship before taking their leave. JC stood at the rail keeping careful tabs on who was going ashore. So far none of the ship's company had left. He assumed that they all had duties in securing the boat for the night. Captain Jack had said that the subsequent cruise had been cancelled due to the delays that had accumulated on this ill-fated voyage.

The Shelbys had just left the dock when Susan looked back and noted, "JC, have a look. Bob seems to be finished with whatever he has to do aboard. I just saw him leave the ship and go off behind that building over there."

"That's probably their workshop area," said JC. "I imagine they have quite an establishment here if they have a large vessel like this to care for. They may have other ships too." He looked around the wooded-lined shore for signs of other docked vessels. "I don't see any others. It must be a pretty small company."

Susan knew they had work to do. "JC, we had better check in with the owner or manager. My guess is that we will be needed by the authorities around here. I don't know whether it will be the local police or the FBI but I'm sure we aren't finished."

JC gave a wry smile, "No, not finished by a long shot." He gestured toward the entrance to what was obviously the main office area. "Let's go on in and introduce ourselves. I would guess that Captain Jack has radioed our presence and role to headquarters. They must be expecting us."

The reception area of the cruise company was really just a small parlor. There was a desk at one end. The two of them went in and looked around for someone to speak to. It wasn't but a moment before a very nice looking woman appeared from an adjoining room. She was casually dressed in working clothes, jeans and a sweatshirt, and was wearing grubby looking sports shoes. Mrs. Pierce was a very fit looking female of a certain age – perhaps fifty or sixty with gray hair pulled back into a ponytail, obviously to get it out of the way when she was working. Clearly she was a hands-on kind of person as far as the business went.

"Hi, I'm Clara Pierce, owner. You two must be the Shelby's. Please sit down." She gestured towards the worn looking couch.

She perched on an occasional chair and said, "You two have had a rather rough voyage I take it."

Susan said, "That's putting it mildly." Then getting into it said, "Have you been contacted yet by the FBI?"

Mrs. Pierce replied, "Yes indeed. They talked to me quite some time ago – since you all were in Buffalo, in fact. I'm pretty well up on the story." She grimaced, "It's a very troubling business. Do you have any ideas to report yet?"

JC said, "We've wracked our brains. This has been the most mysterious series of mishaps that anyone could imagine. We don't really know what to make of it."

"Don't you have some guesses at least?" asked Clara.

Susan said, "Well, I hate to actually come right out and say it but I think I must. You, of all people, should at least know what's on our minds. We keep coming back to Bob Walden. For some reason he seems to be connected to each of the deaths – we have to call them murders at this point. But we know for a fact that he never really seemed to have an opportunity. It really is a necessary requirement. Then there is motive. Why in the world would Bob Walden be in on wiping out the Gunderson clan? It simply doesn't make sense."

Clara Pierce didn't reply immediately. Finally she said, "That is a surprise." Then very reluctantly, "I shouldn't say so, not without more to go on, but I have to say that Bob always came across to me as a little too much 'jolly fellow.' I never really liked him much but then Captain Jack found him to be a first class right-hand man."

Susan started to reply when the tranquility was shattered by the sound of a loud explosion. The three leapt to their feet and then, as if by instinct, JC and Susan threw themselves down on the carpet. They lay there paralyzed for a minute at least when at least Clara spoke. She had remained on her feet.

"That sounded like a shotgun blast. It came from out back - the workshop direction. We had better go have a look. That damned gun. I told Larry not to keep it in the shop. I'll bet they've had an accident."

They all started for the door but JC pushed ahead and said, "Stay back I'm going to have a peek around. We don't know what's going on. Let's be a little careful."

Susan's reaction was beginning to set in. She began to shiver and felt weak in the knees. She had been involved in enough scary scenarios in the past not to recognize this as another crisis - perhaps a dangerous one.

JC crept very quietly along the path leading to the workshop building. All was very quiet at the moment. No one seemed to be around. Clara hadn't made it clear but there didn't seem to be any workmen on the job. Maybe they just weren't needed at present. As far as JC could guess only Bob Walden would have been back here. There had been no sign of life when they had finally left the ship. All the passengers had departed the premises and the college students and the rest of the ship's company were still aboard cleaning the ship. JC went around the side of the building in order to get a view of the inside through a window. Who ever had fired that gun might still be around. Where else could he be? The window was dirty and streaked by recent rains but he was able to make out most of the interior. What he saw caused him to shout out in horror.

"You better get down here Mrs. Pierce. I think it is safe. "We've got a real problem."

A real problem indeed! Inside the three of them were confronted with a sight no one could ever wish to see. There was blood everywhere, splattered on a nearby workbench, the walls, the floor. In the midst of this sea of red lay a body with a gaping hole in the chest. It was Bob Walden, blown out of existence at close range by a very powerful shotgun blast. Next to the body lay the discharged firearm.

JC said, "Mrs. Pierce, call the police." He turned to Susan, "I'm going to contact Agent O'Kelley." Then to the two of them, "We will stay out of here. I suggest we not set foot anywhere near here for the time being. The police will want a clean scene, uncontaminated. It looks like a suicide but then you never know. We can't disturb anything. Let's just go back the way we came and wait."

◊

The wait wasn't long. Soon the place was crawling with police. In addition Siobhan O'Kelley had informed them that she would be there as soon as she could. It wasn't far. She was taking a small government jet to the Providence airport and a car from the local office would bring her on. She said it would be within the next hour and a half.

The FBI agent arrived on schedule and took charge of the investigation. All the material evidence was handled with extreme care. She knew this had to be connected. The case had taken a decidedly bizarre turn. After an hour, she felt that things were well enough under control for her to be able to take a time out and sit down for a conference with the Shelbys. She asked Mrs. Pierce if they could have the use of the office-parlor for a private conference. Clara Pierce was ready to collapse and readily assented. She announced she would be in her bedroom if they needed her.

When they were safely tucked away in the parlor O'Kelley started off, "Do you two have any ideas at this point?"

Susan replied, "We both thought it had to be Bob." Then she gave JC a puzzled look, "Honey, do you think it could be suicide? Maybe he felt we were on his trail."

JC said, "Suicide? No way. It looks a little like he might have shot himself but I would swear to the fact that he would have no reason as far as we could tell – his hands were clean in all those other deaths – and then he's just not the type."

The conference proceeded for the next hour and eventually involved the senior officer of the Rhode Island police. At one point Siobhan O'Kelley took Susan aside for a few private comments. Susan didn't exactly say what they discussed. It didn't matter. The police lieutenant was very insistent on having the Shelbys on hand for the investigation. This was a bizarre situation by any standard and he felt that JC would be of great assistance in their further investigations.

O'Kelley seemed to be okay with this and gave Susan a knowing nod, and turned to the officer and said, "Lieutenant, Mr. Shelby is a naval officer in Intelligence and has been investigating this affair since the beginning. He has all the relevant data you might need. I'm sure he will be glad to stay on for a short while. I would like Mrs. Shelby to carry out a task for me, however. It shouldn't interfere with your work."

The lieutenant was clearly a bit overwhelmed by the situation and gave his assent without thinking. After things settled down arrangements were made for the two of them to stay at a nearby motel.

After a meal that evening at a restaurant across the road from their room Susan announced her plan to JC. She knew it would not go down well.

"JC, I have to make a little trip. I talked it over with Siobhan and she feels I'm the one to do the chore. You are in on it too. Don't worry."

JC was puzzled and not a little worried. These kinds of messages from his dear wife usually preceded dire adventures.

"I know I'm not going to like this. What's up?"

"I have to go to Arizona. I've already checked the flights. It's only for a couple of days and I will be straight back here," she said. "Not only that you may be able to join the party there too."

"What?" he burst out. "What in the world do you need to go to Arizona for?"

"We all agree that I might be the one to give the news to Abe, the one remaining Gunderson. In a way it will be 'good news/bad news' for him. Siobhan felt I was the one to do this. It looks like the forty million will be his," she answered. Susan was leaving a great deal unsaid. She knew full well that JC would raise the roof if he knew the whole story.

JC tried to absorb the shock. "Do you even know where he lives?"

"Well, not exactly," she answered, "but I know it's in Tempe." It really shouldn't be too hard to look him up." She put on her best puppy dog attitude. "I am going on an errand of mercy. Better me than someone else."

JC said with some ire, "If they need a woman to deliver messages, how about Agent O'Kelley? She's a woman, and a pretty cute one at that."

Susan knew better than to rise to that bait.

"I'm off first thing tomorrow morning. You will be able to deal with the police and then come on to Arizona and join me. I could tell that they didn't really need to see me. In fact, I think they hardly noticed I was around." As far as Susan was concerned that closed and settled the matter.

CHAPTER 17 –
ARIZONA

Susan landed at Phoenix at 11:00 AM, rented a car and immediately headed for Tempe, a distance of only five miles. It wasn't' hard to find the address of Abe Gunderson; he was listed in the local phone directory. Apparently he had no interest in excessive privacy. He had nothing to hide. She phoned his house to be sure he was in and told him over the phone that she had some family news to share with him. She asked if she might call and discuss it with him. He was brief but polite and suggested she come around after lunch – about one-thirty.

At the appointed time Susan drove up to a typical upper middle class Arizona desert home. The house was low, had a gently pitched roof, and a garden and landscape of the now popular xeriscape type – mostly rocks and cactus. There was no car in the driveway but then in the desert one would probably use the garage as much as possible. At mid-day the heat is fierce in the summer in Phoenix. Temperatures of 120 would not be a bit uncommon. She wondered if he played golf, or if anyone did at this time of year. It seemed doubtful.

Susan was just a little fearful of this visit but her discussions with Siobhan had reassured her. She approached the door and pressed the bell. It wasn't long before her ring was answered. The door opened and a small man appeared. He had a familiar face, clean-shaven, but definitely like the Gundersons she had come to know. It was hard to compare the image of Avery's face with this one. Avery had sported a full beard. Ed was younger but the family resemblance was clearly there.

"How do you do, Mr. Gunderson - Abe Gunderson is it not? I'm Susan Shelby. I've just come from Rhode Island and I'm afraid I'm the bearer of some distressing news. I've been sent by the family lawyer (that wasn't strictly true but it was the agreed on story). May I come in?"

Gunderson seemed to have little to say. He waved Susan in and gestured toward a seat in the living room. Susan was beginning to feel she had made a great mistake in embarking on this little enterprise. There was something about this man's demeanor that bothered her. Not only that, she really didn't like his looks. Ed had certainly exhibited the general family appearance - rather small in stature, lean – but this man gave her a queasy feeling. She couldn't tell why - something about his looks. She did, of course, enter the large living room and made her way to the overstuffed chair he indicated on the far side of the fireplace. Gunderson stood silently near the front door scrutinizing her. It was definitely unnerving.

"Yes, Mr. Gunderson," she said nervously, "As you may know there has been a series of tragedies ---"

"Mrs. Shelby," he said abruptly, "Let's drop the pretense. I am well aware of what has transpired on the ship. Do keep your seat."

He moved from the entryway toward the entrance to what presumably was the kitchen area.

"I will get us some tea. How would that be?"

Susan nodded nervously as he left the room. She could hear him rattling the metal ware in the kitchen. It was some minutes before he reappeared. There was no evidence of a tray or tea things in his hands. In fact he had his hands clasped behind his back. By now she knew she shouldn't have agreed to this trip. He stepped across the room and stood just a few feet from where she was seated. Even though he was a short man he managed to tower over her as she sat slumped in an overly soft easy chair – one that would be hard to get out of in a hurry. It was then that he revealed what he had brought from the kitchen – a very large and very sharp looking knife.

He pointed the knife menacingly at her and said, "Mrs. Shelby, I can see you have guessed my little secret. I know all about you and your husband."

"Mr. Gunderson, what are you doing? Please put away that knife."

"Mrs. Shelby, Susan, don't they call you? You know too much. You and your husband are a pair of busy bodies. We can't have a fuss here. It would bother the neighbors. Did your husband come with you? I expect he will show up fairly soon if you don't reappear or call on schedule." He shifted the knife to his other hand and stroked his chin in thought. "Now, what should I do?"

Susan was desperate, "You can't get away with this. I know who you are. You are Avery, not Abe. Where is Abe? Did you kill him too?"

The man actually laughed aloud, "Kill dear old Abe? No, that was not necessary. My brother passed on quite naturally – unbeknownst to anyone else, of course."

Susan figured that if she could keep him talking she might get out of this mess alive.

"I see, Mr. Gunderson. You were very clever. You just came here to Arizona when he died and established residence as Abe. No one would be the wiser." He nodded. She continued, "Very clever. Are you a golfer? That seems to be what a lot of folk around here do?"

He frowned at this. "Thinking of buying a little time are you? Let's see," he pondered, "I can do away with you right now and just wait for your dear hubby or perhaps lock you up and wait. No! That wouldn't be a good idea. You might raise a ruckus or escape somehow." He moved a little closer and brandished the knife under her nose. "I think we can just take care of the business here and now.

Then he stepped back. "But let's do the deed in the kitchen, shall we? It's easier to clean up the blood on the kitchen tile. I hate to ruin the carpets in my nice living room."

Susan shuddered. She hoped against hope that her plan had not come completely off the rails.

"Mr. Gunderson, please try to think this through. You really can't get away with this. You'll be caught. If you give it up right now you could probably plead insanity and not only get a reprieve from the worst punishment but maybe a nice cushy hospital spot somewhere." His plea of insanity she knew would certainly be no fabrication.

He shook his head and put on a sorrowful look, "Oh dear, and not have a chance to spend my forty million dollars. No, I couldn't do that. You and your husband will just have to join the rest. I'm rather good at this you know? I've had a deal of practice."

As he moved again toward her the doorbell rang. He gave her a very grim and menacing look and stepped to the door. With the knife out of sight in his left hand behind the door he opened it a few inches to confront the caller. He recognized the person immediately and in spite of her small size he quite taken aback and tried to shut the door on her. She thwarted his efforts and pushed her way in. It was Siobhan O'Kelley and she had a gun in her hand.

"Mr. Avery Gunderson, drop the knife and move back. You are under arrest. I'm an officer of the law, an FBI agent."

He smirked as he stepped back dropping the knife on the carpet, "I know who you are."

With those words he suddenly doubled over and with a horrible grimace on his face fell to the floor.

While this brief exchange was taking place Susan had got up from her easy chair and had edged toward the door next to the fireplace, hoping for a chance to escape. She was relived to see O'Kelley but had some doubts as to the outcome of the ongoing episode. She couldn't help but feel that she had embarked on a very foolish task.

It had all been planned. The FBI agent had assured her that she and her colleagues would be keeping very close tabs on events. They had fitted Susan with a wire and the entire exchange before O'Kelley had rung the bell was now in the records. O'Kelley and several agents from the local office had followed Susan to the house and had stationed themselves quietly surrounding the house.

The figure on the floor had made a few abortive movements but was now quite still. O'Kelley moved into the living room and stood over the now still body of Avery Gunderson.

"Susan, it's okay. I'm afraid we lost him. He had a cyanide capsule apparently. I've seen this before. It's the way cyanide works. I'm not surprised. He was really quite mad. His string of killings was as violent and macabre as any I've ever heard of."

Susan asked, "Where is JC? I thought he was to be here with you."

"He took the flight after yours. I expect him any moment. I have people surrounding the place and they are on the lookout for him. As soon as he gets here we will go into town and leave the clean-up to the locals," said O'Kelley.

Susan had finally gotten control of her feelings and went to the door edging warily past the prone figure. O'Kelley was on one knee looking closely at Gunderson's body.

O'Kelley looked up at her and said, "Susan how about going into the back and see if you can find a clothes hamper. See if there's anything in it." She pulled out a folded black trash bag from her pocket and handed it to her.

Susan knew exactly what to look for. She took the bag and headed for the kitchen. As she passed through she couldn't help but shiver once more at the thought of the man's idea her blood might be all over this particular floor and would need mopping up. *My God, what a monster.* In the laundry room she found what she and O'Kelley hoped would be there. With great care she gingerly managed to get the contents of the hamper she had found there into the new trash bag she had been given.

When she returned to the living room she handed the bag to the agent. "You'll want these. I could smell the gunpowder on them. I'm sure he was wearing them in Rhode Island."

O'Kelley grinned, "Thanks; another nail in his coffin – as if we needed it. I had the gun sent into the lab. We should have a report soon on that analysis by the time we get to the office in Phoenix." She gave Susan an admiring smile, "And thanks for the little bag you gave me that had the dinner napkin in it. I am sure our DNA analysis will show that it was Avery that was at the dinner table that night after Muskegon. It will no doubt match the DNA of the gentleman here on the floor."

It was then that Susan heard a car pull into the drive. She knew it had to be JC. She wasn't too sure how she would handle this. He ought to be used to her adventurous peccadilloes by now. At least she hoped so.

JC didn't exactly burst through the door. There was a dead Mr. Gunderson preventing that, but he did look at O'Kelley for permission to enter and did when she gave him the nod. After a few desperate hugs and kisses between the two of them he managed to get a few words out.

"Okay, sweetheart, what went on in here? It looks pretty grim."

Susan gave an elfish grin and said; "Well I guess I just scared him to death. It's a new power I have." She gave him then a very hard look accompanied by a broad grin. "I think I have the answer. It's the old Sherlockian conclusion; we've used it before – *'when you have eliminated all which is impossible, then whatever remains, however improbable, must be the truth.'*"

JC knew that he was going to have to wait for a real explanation. About that time several other officials of the FBI and local police entered the house and O'Kelley motioned to the pair that it was time to leave.

"Let's go into FBI headquarters in town. We can use the office there to debrief and get most of the facts down for the record."

CHAPTER 18 –
LOOSE ENDS

Siobhan settled herself at the desk in the spacious office while the Shelbys opted to sit as close as possible to each other on the visitor's couch. The agent turned on the recorder and announced the date, time, location, and the parties present. JC felt a little like he imagined a person might feel in an interrogation room at a local police station.

O'Kelley started things off. "Let's hear your view as to what transpired aboard the ship with regard to the group known as 'the Gundersons'."

Susan began the narrative. "There were seven of them. Avery was senior and seemed to be the host and in charge of the proceedings. He was also the first to die. He expired just out of Muskegon. We saw him off the ship for cremation in Manistee."

O'Kelley pressed them on this, "Describe what either of you saw in detail of that event. For example, did either of you ever actually see the dead body?"

JC replied, "Well, apparently not. Here he was, alive and as dangerous as ever. I did help get him down to the mates cabin but then I left immediately by request of Bob Walden."

JC then added, "It surely wasn't all Gundersons. There was Bob Walden. I wonder how he figured in this whole mess?"

Susan said, "That's not too hard. Avery must have offered Walden an enormous cut of the forty million if he would do most of the hard work. I feel a little sorry for Bob. He sure misjudged Avery Gunderson. Clearly Avery was quite mad and never had any intention of sharing out some of that money. Bob Walden was the world's most unlucky and probably most stupid patsy."

O'Kelley said, "I think the thing that caused his distress at dinner had to be pretty genuine from what I've heard. It sounds like Puffer fish to me. But it could have been another chemical that they had sought out to display frightening but harmless symptoms. We'll never know now. The crematorium took care of that. That was a dangerous stunt but if Walden had the antidote they might well have decided the risk was worth it."

Susan then said, "It's clear to me that the two of them had to work as a pair. Walden managed to treat him and get him on his feet that first night and then secrete him for the rest of the trip. He undoubtedly assisted him in the entire scheme. It would be easy for Walden to get him on and off the ship under everybody's noses if he was careful. I imagine he kept him well supplied with food while he was locked up in that cabin. No one ever had occasion to go in there. I would say that the way it ended was simply due to the fact that Avery was not about to give up a share of the spoils."

O'Kelley smiled, "It seems there must have been one more body – the one taken off in Manistee. Surely the undertakers at the crematorium would have noticed if the body had not been dead and convincing." She held up her hand and started ticking off on her fingers. "Let's see, that makes one, two, three … the seven Gundersons including spouses, Bob Walden, and an unknown stiff turned to ash in Michigan. That's a total of nine. Whew! This is worse than war."

Susan said, "I'm a Chicago girl. We have lots of dead bodies lying about. They must have enticed some tramp at Grant Park or found one in an alley somewhere. I don't imagine we'll ever know now. Bob and Avery could easily have gotten such a body onto the ship the day before. That cabin of Bob's down on the lower deck was pretty private. It wasn't really near the captain's and Bob said it was his office. He had a cabin next to it for sleeping. My guess is that that it was Avery's little hidey-hole for the entire trip. Bob just smuggled him on and off the ship as needed along the way."

"What do you come up with for the Cleveland murders?" asked O'Kelley.

JC answered, "I think that is fairly simple. Avery simply was spirited ashore by Bob and made his way to the theatre. Surely by then he could have got rid of his whiskers. Those would have been false. They had to know the play and know that those lights would be turned on at the very end. Some how Avery got into the theatre early and set up the short circuit and the stack of old film in the projection booth next to where Jonathon and Myrtle would be seated." He shook his head in disbelief. "No regard for anyone else's life. They could have lost the entire theatre full of people."

O'Kelley then said, "The Niagara Falls event presents a much more iffy situation. What is your read on that?"

JC said, "It is a problem. If the gas all leaked out before they got to the beach they might have lost control near the rapids. Or an alternate idea is that the gas leaked slowly enough that they had their picnic and had started back when the motor quit."

The agent said, "We can run some tests and see how that works. We certainly don't need it to actually close the case but it would be nice to have it in the record."

JC paused, a little puzzled, "How could they have known the Darlings would get the right boat?"

Agent O'Kelley said, "Don't you remember the place – pretty scruffy? The rest of the boats were all up on blocks in back and looked as though they hadn't been rented in a long time. My bet is that a deal was made with the old lady to get one of them out on the water and more or less ready to go. We'll get back to her. I think she has a bit more to tell us."

Susan suggested, "What if they were poisoned? Avery seemed to be partial to poisons. A slow acting poison could have incapacitated them after the picnic and caused them to simply let their boat go over the Falls."

"Thanks for the suggestion. We will do a post mortem anyway. It will show up if its there," said O'Kelley. She didn't seem to think this was a practical suggestion but then all suggestions were welcome. That's how you get at the truth.

JC asked, "What if the ploy with the gas tank on the boat hadn't worked and they had got safely back?"

The agent laughed sardonically, "I have a feeling Mr. Avery Gunderson had a number of arrows in his quiver. Poor souls; they would have met their end some other way. Gunderson had all the time in the world. The cruise was far from over.

"Ed Gunderson's death seemed to be pretty straight forward – monkshood – aconitine. The erratic behavior was an obvious tip off and then, of course, it was found in his system," continued O'Kelley.

"There is one thing that was maybe not so erratic about Ed's death," said Susan. "His behavior in front of the mirror could be explained another way."

O'Kelley looked very alert at this and raised an eyebrow, "What's that?"

"It's possible," said Susan, "that Ed knew what was going on and became aware of the truth when the poison began to take effect. He may have thought he was talking to Avery when he was looking into that mirror. They are brothers after all. An addled mind might have concluded that Avery himself was standing before him." Susan was quiet for a moment and looked quite grim, near tears actually. "That leaves poor Maude. We don't have a clue. I wonder if we'll ever know? She is one person I really got to know. I'm so sorry about her."

JC gave her hand a squeeze. He was still feeling pangs of guilt about Maude. Agent O'Kelley stood and indicated they would not be needed further for the time being. She suggested they might like to stay a day or two here before heading back. Susan said they had just planned on going back as far a Chicago, back to her folks place. They were asked to leave contact information. There would surely be questions. As they started out the office door a secretary hurried in. She gave JC a quick look.

"Mr. Shelby, there's a phone call for you. It's urgent – from New York."

CHAPTER 19 – POSTSCRIPT

J C picked up the instrument the desk. O'Kelley reached over and pressed the lit button. JC seemed to just listen after he had identified himself. He nodded a few times, grimaced, then smiled. Finally he put the phone down and turned to the two women.

"Guess what? That was a call from the New York police. They've found Maude Snyder, injured but alive. She was found half-naked and severely beaten, unconscious, no ID, in a secluded area of Central Park. She's been at Bellevue since in intensive care in a coma. She just awakened and began asking for JC or Susan Shelby. None of the staff at the hospital had any idea who we were, but they've dealt with situations like this before and got the police in on the act immediately. Apparently the string of murders on the ship was high enough profile so that a fairly large number of people in authority knew a few of the names - including ours."

Susan started to weep. She couldn't bring herself to say anything. She was obviously both delighted and distressed at poor Maude's injuries. Finally she got herself in hand and turned to JC.

"We're going back to New York. We've got to see her."

JC grinned, "Of course, dear, we have an obligation to inform her that she is now forty million richer than she was. She may need a little help around her apartment when she leaves the hospital. We can sign on as temporary home help."

Susan said, "You bet. We'll just stay awhile and get her on her feet again. Thank God!" She heaved a very great sigh.

Siobhan O'Kelley pulled a pad out on her desk and made a few notes.

To no one in particular she said, "I guess old Avery followed her off the ship that rainy night." She looked up at the two and continued, "You know, that old man was in his late seventies, small, very undistinguished looking. He could really go anywhere and no one would notice him."

She had an Irish twinkle in her eye when she said, "Look out in that big bad city. It's a dangerous place."

Susan laughed, "Siobhan, you forget. I'm a Chicagoan, born and bred. It's poor JC here that has to look out. He's a helpless innocent Californian."

THE END

Books by Johnny Mack Hood
Available as e-books or in paper print

◊

The Throttlebottom Chronicles and Other Curious Tales

Dark Matter - (Psychological tale of a serial killer)

Adam's Isle – (Futuristic tale of coming of
age in a world of rising sea levels)

The Body in the Stacks *– (First of the series of
JC and Susan Shelby Murder Mysteries)

A Body at the B and B*

Murder Hawaiian Style*

Dead in the Water*

Cannibal Caper*

Molly's Puzzle*

The Erie Murders*

* - The seven JC and Susan Shelby Murder Mysteries are chrono-
logically related but can be read in any order.